SIMULATION

FAIL

Or

How the Simulation Became Reality

and

Reality Became a Simulation:

A Novel

By Gareth Thomas

First Published in Great Britain in 2021 by Leaf Aden Publishing

Copyright 2021 by Gareth Thomas

ISBN

If this is a Simulation then I apologise for ruining it.

Also by the Author:

Science Fiction:

Sacred Flesh: The War of One

Sacred Flesh: The Fall

Sacred Flesh: Armageddon

The Oracle

Modern Horror:

Chardonnay

Historical/Fantasy:

The Art of Magic: Volume One: The White Lich

Historical Fiction:

Physkon

Available from Lulu.com and Amazon.com in paperback and E-Book formats

"Everything has its wonders, even darkness and silence..."

Helen Keller

The following great minds were direct inspirations for this book:

Douglas Adams, Philip K. Dick, H.G. Wells, Ian M. Banks, Gene Roddenberry, Brain Greene, Michio Kaku, Stephen Hawking

The Author thanks:

The Creators of the Legendary BBC TV Series: Doctor Who, Red Dwarf and The Hitchiker's Guide to the Galaxy.

My mother and father – for their influences in science fiction and efforts reading and correcting the first draft.

My brothers: Matt, Dan and Marcus – whose interest in science fiction and comedy led me to the influences that created this story.

Chapter One

At The End Of The Universe

Let me to take you on a journey to the end of the universe. Before you start panicking and gripping the sides of you seat, allow me to explain: I do not intend to take you physically anywhere, simply transport your imagination through time to the distant end of existence and our final, cold destiny. Let me also reassure you that we will not dwell on the far end of existence for too long – as the infinite darkness that lies there is of no great interest to anyone (least of all the poor souls that are forced to inhabit that lonely epoch).

If we start at the present year and accelerate rapidly through time, we see the world steadily decay. Ancient stone monuments like the pyramids eventually crumble after a million years. Super volcanoes erupt and gigantic asteroids pound the surface. Finally, after almost a billion years, the sun begins to lose luminosity and expand. Photosynthesis fails, wiping out all plant life. The oceans boil.

The Earth is dead.

You might feel that this is a little abrupt, particularly if you have some kind of attachment to this world. Let me assure you that the speed we are accelerating through time means that its entire existence is just an insignificant blip in the grand scheme of things. We will, nonetheless, return there later in the story. For now, it is necessary for you to accept that it has long since faded into obscurity.

Another few billion years pass and the expanding shell of the sun swallows the Earth. It grows into a red giant that encompasses the inner system and then fizzles away into a white dwarf. It ends its life barely any brighter than the moon is today.

That is how our solar system ends, just a few short billion years from now. Its total lifespan was about 10 billion years. We are travelling much further than this, however.

Stars are born and die in the blink of an eye. The remains of our own solar system eventually coalesce into a new sun, with new planets spinning around it. Another opportunity for life blossoms. The universe continues like this for some time, recycling matter and energy whilst all the time growing and expanding. Evolution and extinctions continue in cycles.

Then things start to change.

At the year 46 billion we reach a significant moment. Up until this point, new stars have continued to appear at the edges of the observable universe – more and more stars have time for their light to travel to reach us. As it continues to expand faster and faster, the distant edges of the universe begin to disappear forever. Eventually, the stars that had just appeared suddenly disappear again, shifting away faster than their light could travel. More and more of the previously observable universe fades– never to be seen again. Former colonies, cut off by billions of light years, can no longer communicate with or see their original homes.

The expansion of the universe continues to accelerate.

Intelligent life undergoes a change in philosophy. Formerly warring neighbours suddenly saw a desperately dark, lonely future – cut off from the rest of the universe. They now make friends where they had made enemies. Every intelligent species has a vested interest in surviving the long dark night that they see coming.

Another 100 billion years pass and the universe has changed significantly. New stars are no longer being born. Matter has spread out too far and too thinly to coalesce. One by one the stars in the night sky are going out and they are not being replaced. The long dark night is arriving. When the final sunset arrives, there will be no further dawn.

As the last sun dies, the Age of Starlight comes to an end.

We have entered the Degenerate Era.

This is how the universe will spend most of its existence – cold, dark and lonely. The brief and beautiful era of galaxies, planets and stars was merely a heartbeat long.

We go trillions of years forward and see life desperately attempting to survive this bleak future. There are only black dwarfs, black holes and tiny neutron stars for it to survive around. Energy is a precious resource. Matter is now just fuel to feed their ethereal consciousness.

The combined intelligences of the observable universe work together to survive. They have transcended their combined intellect into digital patterns that float on the remaining waves of energy. Clinging to the supermassive black holes, they transmit themselves across the known universe in an attempt to relay all remaining thought and intellect. It is a desperate attempt to survive until the final Heat Death of the universe.

This is the Alpha Consciousness.

From its original concept are spawned dozens of copies, transmitted to all reaches of space. After a few hundred trillion years it has touched as many parts of the universe that it can ever hope to reach. It spreads like a thin network along gravity waves and energy beams, taking billions of years to communicate with other parts of itself.

This is still not enough.

The black dwarfs are gone. All remaining matter in the universe evaporates. All that is left are the black holes and even these are beginning to fade away. As they get smaller they release more and more energy, feeding the desperate consciousness on their border. Finally, they burn out and explode, lighting the infinite darkness in a brief but spectacular firework.

This is the Black Hole Era: The final stages in the immensely long lifespan of reality. The largest of their kind will continue to evaporate for trillions upon trillions of years. But they have a definite lifespan: The universe is finite.

Once the last supermassive black hole dwindles into nothing, the universe would be dead.

Time will become meaningless.

No matter.

No energy.

Nothing.

This is the problem that we face at the end of the universe.

We are not going that far, however. We will stop during the earlier phase of the Black Hole Era. The Year is Half a Googol (50 x 10 to the power of 50). Or to put it another way:

50,000,000,000,000,000,000,000,000,000,000,000,000,000,000,000, 000,000,000,000,000,000,000,000,000,000,000,000,000,000,000,000 and one.

The conversation was already going on for far too long.

It was a conversation that could have echoed through time from another age. It was the conversation of a project manager and their programmer. It was the conversation of a manager and their worker. It was a subordinate being berated for failing to do something their superior was incapable of.

It should have been a simple update – checking the original program against various Beta Tests. The problem was that all of the checks were coming in with the same problem. It was an obvious problem, something so clear that all of the testers were noticing it straight away.

The program stated that the universe ended at some point around its sixteen-billionth birthday. It clearly had not, otherwise the very program that it was running could not have been designed.

If you cannot get the program to function correctly, a new Integrated Consciousness will be brought online to take over the project.

That was what the Alpha Consciousness had said. The threat in the statement left no uncertainty that her very existence was on the line, along with that of her 'child'. Their single raison'd'etre was to ensure the successful implementation of the program. If they failed in this task they would no longer be required.

Omega would survive.

The problem was that existence had a very finite length of time attached to it. The universe was cooling and expanding. Along with the fundamental rule that nothing could travel faster than light, there were several other long held science fiction tropes that experimentation over trillions of years had proven or disproven. Time travel, as another example, was found to be impossible – not only for reasons of logic, but clear physical reasons as well. Quantum physics had proven beyond a doubt that things travelling in the opposite direction in time were inverted in state – meaning that if they had existed going forwards, they could not exist going backwards.

Most species stopped tampering with time travel when they ran into this brick wall. One did not and managed to wipe themselves out by attempting to transport their whole civilization back in time to escape a solar catastrophe.

With both light speed and time travel impossible, Life had to find other ways around the physical limitations of the universe. As the universe passed middle age, this search became their driving obsession.

Omega was one of the final steps of this universal goal.

Omega was the programmer. Or rather, she was an amalgamation of programmers. The final goal was to make a simulated universe – from the moment of creation to its final dying gasp. It was designed with the collective observations of as much of the universe as they could gather. When added to their understanding of the laws of physics, they would be able to extrapolate the entire life of the universe into a single digitized program.

At least, that was the plan.

In order to create this grand digital universe for them to play in, she had to construct a suitably advanced intelligence to run it. This was her baby; the sole endeavour of her immense intellect. She had effectively birthed an entirely new artificial intelligence, so advanced that it could maintain a simulation of the entire life of the universe.

Once complete, they could experience all of existence at their leisure. It would be like an infinite playground for all of the surviving intelligences to enjoy. Time would run at a speed that would slow with the dwindling power available left in the universe. As the last gasp of energy dripped from the last possible release of electrons, the program would slow to its final infinite moment. For those within, it would stretch for infinity – whilst the universe itself could trundle on towards its finite end without interfering with their perception of the passing of that time.

It would have been perfect.

It was a grand task and the consciousness of Omega was more than aware of the importance placed on it. She was basically responsible for the survival of all existence. She did not need the Alpha consciousness berating her about how the program was not working.

The universe did not end in the year sixteen billion.

That one comment had taken several billion years to cover the distances between them and did nothing to help solve the problem. So far, the conversation had taken almost sixteen billion years – which Omega was tempted to point out as ironic. It would take a further billion years for the witticism to reach Alpha, though – by which time the point would have been lost.

She had not wasted the sixteen billion years since the problems had started. So far, she had managed to extrapolate several incongruities in the failures. Not all of them collapsed at the year sixteen billion – though it was definitely the majority. There were a few tests that did not last much longer than eight billion years and even one that dropped as early as two billion – not long after sentient life first developed. There was a further spike at around thirteen and a half billion years and then a steady increase until it reached the age of sixteen billion. She spent her time studying these points in the simulation.

The graphs were a great help to visualize the problem, but Alpha had been at pains to point out that it did not get them any closer to a solution.

Omega had identified as a female, even though the amalgamation of her consciousness was so mixed that any form of gender identification was an indulgence. There was no body that she inhabited, nor any physical characteristics that she could identify with. Her reasoning lay in the fact that she, alone, of all the collective consciousnesses that existed at this remote corner of time, had been brought to life to give birth to a digital universe. As the mother of all of creation (albeit digital), she felt it appropriate to approach the task with as much motherly instinct as she had available. Consequently she was very protective towards her young, beautiful program. It was her child. In turn, it would eventually give birth to a place for all of creation to continue.

Alpha was the first amalgamation of consciousness – the centre of their collective existence at the end of reality. It held all of the data on all of the surviving species, keeping their individual minds stored in a digital ether. When the time came, they would be plugged into the completed program and allowed free reign of their own individual universes – built from a precise model of reality. A model that Omega's child would have designed for them. Until then, Alpha was effectively the manager for the universe.

She imagined it identified as male.

The first test to return had been a disappointment, but she had still held to the belief that this was just a minor slip and that her child would perform brilliantly overall. It was expected that some parts of the program would glitch on their first run. One failed test did not sour the whole program.

Then a second report, a third, fourth, fifth and more came in – all repeating the errors of the first and showing that it was a fundamental issue with the child. Some of the consciousnesses echoing in her psyche could recall biological children with mental and genetic issues. There were mothers within her that were conjuring images of large headed, wide-eyed babes of a dozen species. All of them had different, haunting defects. Just like her child.

I will get it working again. These are just a few teething problems. The majority of the tests should come back successful.

These were the first comments she had sent back to Alpha, whilst at the same time receiving more and more errors. As those mounted inevitably towards a hundred percent failure, she had received the first in a trail of sarcastic and semi passive-aggressive responses from Alpha:

The majority of the tests have been failures.

That had taken a billion years to get to her and in that time *all* of the tests had been confirmed as failures. The rest of the sixteen billion year discussion had followed similar lines.

Less than a second had passed since she had sent her final message and in that time her massive intellect had come up with a solution. She considered it quite simple and possibly enjoyable to fix:

She would access the program at the point of collapse, ascertain what triggered it and then stop it.

Simple.

It was only as her consciousness was downloading into the program that the weight of her problem truly started to dawn:

She needed to save the universe.

Chapter Two

The Universe Ends

His day was not going well. Little did he know that it was about to get significantly worse. In fact, there would be no worse day after this one. There would also be no other days after this: This would be the last day.

The universe was exactly sixteen billion years old. This was not a significant date for him, but as you will already be aware, it was an extremely significant age for this particular simulated universe. It is important that you remember that his existence is within a purely constructed reality – as the rules of physics do not work in the same way here as they do in the 'real world'. This will have increasingly revelatory results for Omega later on, but for the moment it should be sufficient to explain her coming frustrations.

His experience of this day was noteworthy because of its unfortunate and confusing passage. For your benefit, we join Raxus Pross later on in that day. We will explain his earlier frustrations after first exploring his trial. At this point he has already met Omega, but we will return to that point later on as her passage in and around the program during these early moments is difficult to track.

Raxus was currently standing before his peers, desperately trying to explain to them why he might need the piece of equipment that he had not yet stolen.

This was just one of the problems with time travel. You will come to see some of the many reasons it is not possible in the real universe but is unfortunately necessary within the simulation. Omega had designed it in such a way that she and her cohabitants at the end of the universe could occupy any period of its existence - there would have been little point if all they could do was experience the universe in the same epoch that they presently occupied in reality: There was nothing left there but black holes and continually expanding empty space.

The simulated universe which Raxus occupied was not only filled with matter, stars and life, but was also host of many physical impossibilities that could not exist in reality. It would have been a very interesting place for Omega and her people to occupy, if it was not about to collapse.

The simulated room that he happened to be occupying was hexagonal in shape, with raised podiums sprouting from each corner. The centre was dipped in a slightly sloped pit, one that he could easily walk out of if he needed to. His tribunal was made up of eight beings, each of them linked to the central matrix via invisible augments. They spoke, listened and judged as one.

"If the projections are correct, then it will not matter if I take the device or not," he was arguing. "The universe is going to end. It will not matter at what point in time I take the device. It will still end, just the same."

"These projections are still under debate," came the unified response from his peers. "It cannot be certain that the universe will end until that moment comes to pass."

This was surprisingly true. They had already established the true age of the universe. Their best projections showed that it would go on to live many more hundreds of billions and trillions of years before finally and completely dying out. It was only his new projections that painted the stark and sudden prediction that it would end today. Unfortunately his evidence was both convincing and (as we know) true.

"I repeat my point," he sighed, turning on his heel to face the entire room. "If there is nothing to fear, then why am I on trial?"

"You will take the device if we do not interfere," was the cold response. "As its taking will be illegal, we have no choice but to convict you for this potential action."

"You know as well as I do - that may not even prevent me taking the device!" he objected, adding; "and you will cause a paradox by preventing the action that you know would happen from taking place!"

"The minor paradox created by the prevention of your actions has been deemed insignificant in comparison to the major paradox that would be caused if you did take the device. Severe fluctuations in the time vortex ripple from this action."

"Probably because the universe is about to end," he commented, drily.

"You have already been found guilty of committing the crime."

He knew how futile his position was. He had seen others put on tribunals for very similar reasons. There was never any way of professing your innocence as you had already committed the crime in their eyes. They simply travelled back in time to a point before you did it and then incarcerated you. It meant that any form of rebellion was impossible.

This leads us into how his day had started and how it had got to the point of him being accused of committing a crime in a future that would soon not exist.

Raxus was not a rebellious man by nature. He was more of a theorist. Most of his days were spent calculating ridiculously complicated formulae. His field was in the '*effects of minor paradoxes on the structure of pocket dimensions*'. This innocuous title should have held some gravitas, as it was an area designed to investigate how long they could maintain their existence.

This requires some explanation: Raxus's simulated universe was a lot more dangerous than the real one that had spawned it.

They existed within a bubble universe, offset from the main one (which was actually the simulated one, but nobody in this universe was yet aware of that). They lived in this bubble to protect themselves from the monstrous threats that his universe had created: His universe was fighting a Time War, a War with the Multiverse and was also gripped by an invasion of cyborg monstrosities called Hybrids. It was a dangerous existence outside of the bubble. Every day held the threat that their little bubble universe could come crashing down on them for any number of reasons.

Most days its did not. The days that it did, it relapsed back into days where it didn't - due to the time travelling nature of its defenders. Sometimes it was in such a quantum state of existing and not existing, it made it impossible for its enemies to be able to coordinate an attack.

His normal daily life began by downloading into a fresh organic receptacle. This was followed by an injection of vitamins and neural electrolytes to hone the brain and bodily functions. Then he was transmitted instantaneously to his laboratory, deep inside a bunker in a further artificial dimension. This was so that he could then safely form test situations completely removed from the universe they inhabited.

Yes, this makes it a pocket laboratory dimension within a bubble dimension within a simulated dimension from the mind of an AI made in the actual universe.

This fact will become more important later on. For now, just make sure you are aware of how many artificial realities are involved: It's four.

His laboratory could take any form that he wanted, as he had complete control of its bubble universe. At present he had no real need for anything more complicated than a calculator and a whiteboard. He did indulge himself a little more than that and the white board was a holographic display that reacted to his hand signals. The calculator was an integrated computer system that made calculations augmented with his brain.

His tests had led him to the conclusive belief that the effects of paradox were far worse than previously predicted. The universe was on the brink of a complete collapse.

Every number he had crunched, every way he had tried to bend the math, led him closer and closer to the terrifying (and as we know, correct) conclusion.

The universe was about to end.

It was not an easy conclusion to come to and had been the first contribution to the plight of his day. Watching result after result come through stating that you were about to die was never easy. Coupling this fact with the ending of all of existence, it significantly soured his mood.

Next would be the hardest part of his career: Explaining the problem and convincing his peers of the evidence. We will gloss over this endeavour later in his day, as it takes place during his tribunal and we have already seen his attempts were completely fruitless. We will focus instead on what exactly his job involves:

There had been paradoxes ever since the (simulated) universe had something to fight over. The earliest species known to leap through time had attempted to eliminate all competition by wiping out all other life at the start of the universe. This would have left them alone and dominant in the universe as the only form of life to have ever existed. All they managed to do was create a major paradox event that prevented anyone else from going to the same time period. Several other species had pulled similar stunts throughout the Time War (stretching up and down the timeline). Generally speaking, the other species would step in to stop too much damage from taking place – the Chronobots specifically taking a particular affront to any form of paradox. The Hybrids, however, did not care for the dangers to the structure of reality and had been the worst players in the Time War. The effect of their careless time travel and alterations to the timeline were tearing their parent universe to pieces. There were fractures, collapses and splinters all the way through time – each contributing towards the overall structural failure that Raxus was predicting. This was shown in a variety of elaborate and colourful patterns on his holographic white board.

"That does not look good," a voice had interrupted his thoughts.

"What are you doing here?" he asked, swinging around to face the intruder. "This laboratory should be sealed!"

The figure that stood before him did not seem to care for the fact that she should not have been in there. She had her hands in her pockets and a slightly bemused expression, whilst staring over his shoulder into the scrawl of his calculations. She was stunningly attractive, but then most people chose their organic receptacles to be good looking. Only a few people ever wanted to look ugly – and that was usually a warning that their mood was something similar.

The second thing he noticed about her was the fact that she seemed to be dressed in the same clothes as him. It was as if she was not sure what she should wear and consequently copied his exactly.

She had ignored his question and continued to stare over his shoulder at the hologram and his calculations.

"You know that this is not the cause, don't you?" she asked pointing towards one of the fundamental parts of his formulae.

"I am sorry, who are you?" he asked, swinging between the projection and her with increasing anger.

"I am part of the administration," she explained evasively. "Call me Omega."

This may have been true, as the only others who could have transported into his bubble lab would have been members of the university faculty. Even then, they should not be barging into people's labs without prior warning or invitation. If he had been conducting an experiment it could have been dangerous for both of them.

This fact made him more angry and he began to puff himself up and throw an accusatory finger at her.

"Listen, *Omega*, I do not know how you got in here, but this should be a sealed laboratory."

"I think you should be more worried about what your calculations are saying," she responded, ignoring his increasingly flustered responses. Her attention was now almost entirely on the formula he had projected.

"And what makes you an expert on the collapsing wave functions of paradox events?" he shot, angrily. She looked across at him, raising an eyebrow.

"Paradox events?" she asked, as if she had never heard of them before.

"That's what the calculation is!" he erupted, as if he was now convinced this was a charade. "What are you doing here?!"

"Well its not the reason for the collapse," Omega shook her head. "There is another huge force occurring. If you look at this part, its only making up two percent of the total."

"What are you talking about?" he growled, angrily. "You are not making sense. My calculations are perfect."

"They aren't perfect. They are good. I think I see why I thought you would be useful."

He stared at her as she slowly drew herself back from his calculations and looked him over. It was the cursory look that someone might give a side of beef that they had spotted for their dinner. It did nothing to make him feel better about who she was or what she was doing in his laboratory.

"I think you need to leave."

"So do you," she stated. "If you believe what you have scrawled, then the universe will start collapsing any moment."

"What are you doing here?" he asked, trying a new tack. She clearly knew about his work, but he was not aware of any 'Omega' in the university faculty. He certainly did not like the way she looked at him, the fact that she had got into his sealed lab nor the way she had referred to herself as part of the 'administration'.

"I like your work," she winked at him. "It could be useful for me."

"Useful for you? If we are all about to die, how can it be useful to anyone?!"

"Good point," she nodded, as if the universe ending did not really matter to her. "Don't dwell on that fact, if I were you."

He stared at her, wondering if she was mad. Or maybe he was mad and she did not exist. Flaws in organic receptacles were rare but not unheard of. His consciousness could have been downloaded into one with an unnoticed brain injury...

"I better go," she interrupted his frantic thoughts. "You have friends on the way."

With that she tapped a device on her arm a few times and promptly disappeared.

It was not the kind of surge of energy and dispersal that he was accustomed to. Usually someone would flash with light and there would be a suck of air from where their body had been. All of that was typical of a transporter beam. She did none of this and simply disappeared without a trace of her being there.

He immediately stepped up to where she had been standing and looked around, as if it would help him work out where she had gone/come from.

Then there was a flash of light and a suck of air as he also disappeared.

The laboratory faded away and a heartbeat later he was standing in the entrance portal. The transporter beam faded away with a momentary whirr.

There were three people standing before him, each looking down their noses at him.

"You closed my lab?" Raxus asked, confused. He recognized one of them as his project manager. The other two, he soon found out, were there for his tribunal.

So his day then took another lurch towards the worse. They were not there to listen to his terrifying hypothesis and evidence of the universe ending. They were not there to investigate the strange woman that had appeared in his laboratory. They were there to arrest him for something he had not even done yet.

It was a humiliating experience. He was escorted out of the faculty and transported to the tribunal. A group of his peers were chosen to connect to the matrix and judge him. By the time those peers had been chosen, everyone in the faculty was aware of his arrest.

"Your protestations about the end of the universe does nothing to help alleviate your crime. If anything, it provides us with a motive."

"That's not how the collapse works," he sighed, shaking his head in exasperation. "Its a complete collapse. There will be nowhere... No *when* you can hide in."

"Regardless of this," the tribunal continued in one eerie voice, "you have been found guilty of the crime already. Your punishment has been decided and you will be incarcerated."

"For how long?" he sighed, knowing full well that the universe would end long before he was released.

"The correctional matrix has deigned that three days will be all that is needed to ensure the crime cannot be committed."

He sighed. Under any other circumstance a three day incarceration would be a death blow to a career. With the universe ending imminently, it suddenly felt like it was menial.

"The tribunal is adjourned."

The seven peers all detached themselves from their consoles and looked down on him in unison. Avoiding their gazes, he slowly made his way back up the sloped floor towards the doorway. At this point, he felt as if his day would not be able to get any worse.

He may be right. It was certainly about to get more confusing.

The first thing to occur was the sudden collapse of the bubble universe that they were inhabiting. This was almost unnoticeable from within and only a slight blur revealed that anything had happened at all. From outside the bubble, it was as if it had spontaneously exploded and then instantaneously reformed exactly the way it had been.

This was the first sign of an attack.

The room erupted into alarms and suddenly the tribunal were transporting away. Within moments Raxus was left alone.

A deep rumble echoed through the facility, as if an earthquake or aftershock was vibrating through its artificial floor.

Omega appeared, looking far more worried than she had been earlier. She looked at the shaking walls and then down at the strange device on her wrist. A moment later her look of worry had switched to determination.

"It has begun," she stated to him. "We need to leave."

"I am not going anywhere with you," he responded. "Not until you explain who you are."

She paused, held out a hand and smiled at him.

"I need your help."

"That does not answer my question," he replied, coldly. "Kindly explain why you are wearing the same clothes as me and how you keep appearing and disappearing like that."

She looked at his garments and then across at hers, wondering for a moment why they were not acceptable. A moment later she was shifting the device on her wrist to project another, random set of clothes picked from one of the more widely available images of humans in her database. There was one particular set that was both appealing and appeared in a huge array of photographs. She assumed that this would be acceptable.

The lace lingerie she now appeared in seemed to make Raxus more uncomfortable. He shook his head and tried to look away.

"Maybe you were better off just copying me," he mumbled. She had chosen a particularly attractive body to inhabit and some particularly alluring lingerie. One of his eyes could not help but stare.

A moment later her former clothing was reappearing over her, matching his own garments.

"What the hell are those?" she asked, stepping back from him, suddenly. Noticing her stare was directed over his shoulder, he slowly began to turn around.

The Chronobots were notoriously passive most of the time. They only ever seemed to become active or interfere in anything when paradox was involved. It was believed that they had some fundamental interest in preserving space-time. As this was in everyone's best interest, they were seldom confronted. Every time-faring civilization had their run ins with them at some point – usually during the opening moments of them entering the time stream. Many did not survive that initial encounter and ended up being relegated to a point where they never developed time travel. Others were wiped out by the Elder Civilizations (like the Magua) – who all initially loathed the idea of other species.

Then there were the Hybrids.

These were the only species that the Chronobots did not interfere with, despite them being the worst culprits for causing paradox.

The Chronobots were bizarre clockwork robots that seemed to be held together by will. There were no joints and each cog and wheel seemed to float around its innards in a constantly shifting array of moving parts. Nobody knew where they came from, who made them or for what purpose.

The Hybrids were cyborgs of a variety of species, all unified through augmented brain functions into a sinister matrix. This one had once been a humanoid, from a branch of humanity that had left Earth over a billion years before. The similarity to Homo sapiens ended after the two arms and legs, however. It had cybernetic eyes, huge, spiked shoulders and an array of equipment over its torso. It had no mouth nor nose but a huge, single ear-like sensor device that stretched around its cranium. Finally, its skin was bristling with needle like weapons – some that fired physically into their prey, others that focused weapons or shielding around it. They swept through the universe like a plague, determined to unify all life as one. If Omega had been aware of their philosophy, she may have seen a direct similarity with her own existence: an amalgamation of many species' consciousnesses into one integrated matrix.

Raxus, however, did not explain any of the above and instead dove into her in an attempt to get out of their line of fire. She was still pointing at the strange pair of creatures when he hit her. She lost her footing on the sloped floor and the two of them tumbled and slid back down to the base of the room.

The Hybrid lowered its needles towards them – thousands of tiny, sharp devices ready to be fired. The Chronobot pointed and the Hybrid suddenly disintegrated.

"Universe One must be maintained," the Chronobot stated, as if it was explaining its actions.

Omega decided not to take any chances. She shifted the device on her wrist and deleted the part of the simulation that held the Chronobot. It seemed to whine and then simply disappeared.

Raxus stared. He was confused by the Chronobot destroying the Hybrid. He was at a loss as to what she had just done. Most of all, he was thoroughly terrified by the fact that they all seemed to be just appearing and disappearing at will.

"What is going on?" he pleaded, staring at where the Hybrid had been standing.

"This is the start of the collapse," she replied, rising back to her feet and checking the device on her wrist. The alarm was still going and there were more rumbles echoing from within the facility.

"What is that thing on your arm?" he asked, pulling himself up.

"That would take some explaining. We probably don't have the time right now."

"You still haven't explained who you are. You are not part of the university faculty."

She looked up from the device and threw him a grin.

"No. I said I was part of the administration."

"And what is that supposed to mean?"

"Look, this is probably going to come as a shock to you, but this universe is not real. It is artificial."

He stared at her like she had just stated the obvious.

"I know," he replied. That made her look up from her device and stare at him, intently.

"What?!" she exclaimed, grabbing him. "You know it is a simulation?"

"No..." he shook his head, wondering what she meant. "The simulated universe is in the other faculty. This one is our home bubble. The one we built to escape the Time War..."

She stared at him in horror. There were several parts of that statement that worried her. He cocked his head at her, wondering what he had said to concern her so.

"This universe is artificial?" she asked, still processing the other worries.

"Of course it is."

"And your laboratory. That was artificial?"

"Yes. An artificial universe inside our bubble one."

"How many of these universes have you created?" she asked, checking her device and starting an algorithm to add this new information. The simulated universe should never have simulated more universes than were present in her home one. She could no loner be sure how many simulations were being maintained. Raxus had told her that it was a bubble inside their simulated universe, but there could be more beyond that.

"Wait... you said the simulated universe was held in another faculty?" she asked. "What did you mean?"

"Yes. Its the flagship project for the university," he nodded. "Its goal is to create a complete simulation of the universe – beginning to end."

She sighed. That answered that question: there were lots more.

"How?" she asked, ignoring the continuing rumbles of nearing explosions.

"We created an artificial universe to hold a program big enough to run the simulation."

"I had a feeling it would be," she sighed, finally lowering the device on her wrist. If she was right, it was about to become useless to her. If she was right, the problem could be a lot worse than what she had feared.

The universe may be lost.

Her child might have to die.

"Take me there," she demanded, though she already knew where it was.

It was at the heart of the collapse.

Chapter Three

Escaping the Collapse of Reality

The University Universe, or Double U (to be more confusing), was not the only artificial universe they had created. Nor were they the only species making these artificial universes. There was no way of knowing how many others had been created. Nor was there any way of knowing how many her AI had created aside from the one that it was supposed to have made.

She could not calculate the speed of the collapse without knowing how many artificial realities existed. It could well go on for infinity – as more and more of these artificial, simulated universes created further artificial simulations of their own in a never ending blossom of existence.

However, none of this explained why they were all simultaneously ending.

Omega tried to ascertain what Raxus had been studying and get an idea of the maths behind the paradox effects. Where she came from, Time Travel was impossible – therefore an in depth knowledge of paradox and its effects were not necessary. There were, however, several theoretical mathematicians that had dabbled with the idea over the near half a googol years of her amalgamated consciousnesses. This was enough for her to follow what he was saying and admit that there was definitely some evidence that he was right. Also, she knew that the universe was about to end.

Time Travel had to be possible within the simulation – it was how Omega could drop into it at any point. In fact, she already had done so a few times – skipping all around that final day to try and get as much information from the epicentre of the collapse.

She had first met Raxus a while after after he left the tribunal. As we know, he first met her in his laboratory some hours before.

We were following how Raxus's day was getting progressively worse as the end of his universe approached. We will now look at how Omega first arrived within the simulation, how she met Raxus and how it leads to him committing the crime he has already been convicted of.

The simulation was as perfect looking as she could have hoped for.

It was not Omega's first time inside her creation – she had 'play tested' the Beta version before sending it out to the rest of her universe. Those had only ever been sealed constructs, though – tiny parts of the overall whole. To see the whole thing running at the peak of its life was a beauty to behold.

It was unfortunate that it was in the process of collapsing.

The epicentre of the collapse was based around a particular branch of humans, now regarded as Homo-Superior or 'Celestials'. She had not paid much attention to their history and instead just chose to depend upon her general knowledge of the universe's history. Her long life had left her with some intimate knowledge of humanity. Some of their later civilizations had survived long enough to be included in her consciousness. There were even digital recordings of early twenty first century social media, though none of this was in any way useful.

She chose a form that they would find attractive and then materialized at the heart of the collapse. Unfortunately she did not think to clothe the form she had chosen – as such things were now as alien to her as hats are to a toaster.

The University Universe Hall was already falling apart when she appeared.

The roof of the hall had cracked and through its shattering, disintegrating tiles was an equally splintered sky. Through the gaps were floods of shapes, entering into the distorted landscape like a swarm of flies. Each of these shapes seemed to be firing randomly across the ground – only met by an occasional beam from the surface. They blossomed in fiery explosions wherever they met the ground or sky.

There was a war going on outside.

She was not aware of any wars that should have been going on at this particular moment in time – there certainly had not been anything like this in her history. But then her history did not abruptly end sixteen billion years into its existence.

The hall was an artificial marble construction with layers of bio-luminescence for lights and an array of holographic displays that could be called up anywhere around the room. There were a pair of locals who were currently staring through holograms at her, clearly disturbed by the fact that she was not wearing any clothes. She stared back at them with equal surprise at their garments – wondering what could have possessed them to cover their bodies with coloured fabrics. A memory of some of her more ancient consciousnesses pointed out that it was quite normal for organic creatures to wear clothes – they just hadn't needed them since becoming an amalgamated intelligence.

At this point Raxus entered the hall and skidded to a halt on the marble floor. He stared at her in shock, surprise and confusion.

"Where did your clothes go?" he asked, staring at her naked body.

"Who are you?" she shot back at him, wondering why one of her simulations was recognizing her.

"You told me to get here as quickly as possible," he stated. "You said you needed to do something."

"I say a lot of things," she grumbled – finally deciding to do something about the fact that she was naked. Shaking off this menial embarrassment, she started to tamper with the device on her wrist.

"Who are you?" she asked, again.

"It's me – Raxus. Have we not met yet?"

"Clearly not. What do you do, *Raxus*?" she asked. Finishing with her device, she projected a set of clothes across her that matched what he was wearing. She assumed that this would be acceptable.

"I am a researcher..." he replied hesitantly. "I work in another department..."

Being quite used to the complications created by Time Travel, it was not hard for him to accept that this was the first time she had met him but not the first time he had met her.

Where she came from, time travel was impossible. Hopping into the simulation at any point of her choosing was not.

"I told you to come here?" she asked, looking around the huge marble hallway.

Before he could continue the confusing conversation, everything spontaneously started to contract.

It was as if the entire universe suddenly started to get smaller. If they could have observed themselves, they would have realized they were also rescinding into nothing – just at a slightly slower rate than the larger things. The sky was the fastest to drop, the huge university building the next and then the smaller parts within.

This disparity in the speed of collapse allowed a precious few moments for both Raxus and Omega to react.

Raxus cowered to the floor, placing his hands over his head as the contracting roof disrupted the marble of the not quite so rapidly collapsing walls. The slower shrinking floor tipped the walls and within seconds the entire room was falling inwards on itself, rapidly followed by the dropping sky.

Omega tampered with the device on her wrist and suspended the simulation. The room froze, with only her moving about within it. Outside, the rest of the bubble universe also stopped – remaining fixed until she chose to release it. Outside that bubble universe was the rest of the simulated universe – which continued to collapse. If she had been aware of it at this moment in time, she may have done something about it. Unfortunately, she was not yet aware and could therefore do nothing to prevent it.

This would have dire consequences once she caught up with herself in Raxus's time line.

Realizing that she had already placed some importance on Raxus, she then travelled back through the simulation to the point when she had met him in his laboratory. This confirmed that she was right to want to use him. The collapse that was happening later on that day would not take long to echo back through time to where they were. She estimated that they had a few hours at most before this section of time would also begin collapsing.

She next hopped forwards to test this hypothesis. If she was correct then she would send him into an increasingly packed hall as more and more of him reached the point of collapse and were suspended.

Unfortunately, as the collapse was still continuing through the parent simulation universe, the Raxus that she had initially sent to the hall no longer existed. As time progressed towards that point, the collapse rolled back towards them at an accelerating rate.

This brings us to her appearing at the end of his tribunal.

The collapse began almost immediately – confirming that her calculations were wrong.

That was when he had told her that they were in an artificial universe and she realized she had only suspended the collapse in the bubble. She had not suspended the collapse of the parent simulation universe. In fact, there was no way of knowing if she could.

"So your simulation was made to calculate the entire universe – including all these little bubble realities?" she asked him, trying her best to ignore the increasing rumbles from the war outside.

He nodded, trying his best to focus on her and not the devastation being wreaked on his home.

"And the simulation must have created a simulation of itself – as it is now included in the total of your universe?" she continued.

"My universe?" he asked, shaken by how she had said it. "Its yours, too. Isn't it?"

She ignored his query and asked the question again.

"Yes," he replied, his attention suddenly drawn away by a nearby explosion. "I suppose it must. It's not really my field."

"So it could be spawning an infinite number of simulations?"

"I can't see how... it's still going to have a finite amount of resources to simulate it through."

"Unless it was creating artificial simulated universes to run the calculations..." she growled – which was exactly what her program seemed to be doing.

It was like finding out her child had spawned an unknown number of children who had in turn gone on to have kids of their own. She wasn't sure if she should be proud of the tribe she had made or afraid of it.

By the time they were outside of the tribunal, the sky was cracking like it had when she had first arrived. Hybrids swarmed through those holes, unleashing fire and fury from the heavens. Raxus slowed as the building began to contract again. The roof began to crumble and as it shrank faster than the walls it was being supported by, it inevitably collapsed.

She suspended the simulation again – this time fully aware that the collapse was going to continue.

She needed Raxus alive – he had a grasp of paradox that her consciousness could only dream of. Whatever was causing the collapse was definitely tied to his studies – thus his ability to make the prediction. She could just pluck him out from an earlier point in his timeline, but each time she interfered like this she was creating further paradoxes within the simulation. This just multiplied her problem.

She had no choice. Raxus was already technically gone – his earlier incarnation having been deleted in the collapse at the hall when she first arrived. She was already creating a paradox by interacting with him here, earlier in his timeline.

One more paradox would not make a lot of difference.

She tampered with the device and a moment later both of them were reappearing where they were, some hours before. The universe stopped being paused, but the sky was no longer splitting and the ground no longer shaking. By her estimate, they had a few minutes before the collapse began again at this point in time. There was no way of being sure as she could not predict the number of universes that were collapsing in on them.

Raxus looked up again as time returned to normal and the universe carried on around them again. The roof was no longer collapsing and he no longer needed to cower and cover his face. Lowering his hands from protecting his head, he looked sheepishly over to Omega.

The device on her wrist was sparking in an array of colours, causing her to hold it away from her face. As it finally smouldered into a dormant, smoking ruin, she was left staring at it with a growing sense of dread.

Something was seriously wrong.

"When are we?" Raxus asked – quickly adjusting to the idea that they had travelled in time rather than space.

"A few hours earlier," was her distracted response.

"What happened to the thing on your wrist?"

She tapped it a few more times and then looked away from it, helplessly.

"Shunting you out of your timeline has shorted it out," she growled. "Something is seriously wrong."

"You do know that what you're doing is illegal?" he asked, referring to the fact he had just been put on trial for unsolicited time travel. She just glared at him.

"We need to get further back," she stated, instead. "The rate of collapse is too quick here. I barely have enough time to gather the data before everything falls apart."

"What do you mean?"

"Your universe is collapsing. It starts at the point you predicted and is echoing all the way back to the beginning of time. If we do not act fast then none of your universe will be left to preserve."

"My universe?"

"We do not have time for this at the moment," she growled. "We need to get out of here before the collapse begins. The future is already collapsing. The timeline you came from has already disintegrated."

"How am I still here?" he asked, patting himself down to make sure he was. "If my timeline has collapsed I should have ceased existing with it."

"I copied you into an earlier time. You basically side-stepped it."

It would lead to far too many questions if she had explained that his universe was a simulation and all she did was copy his data into an earlier part. He understood time travel, so she kept with that analogy. Unfortunately he also understood paradox in time travel.

"You made another paradox!" he objected. "That's what is causing the collapse!"

"No," she shook her head. "It's not helping, I admit. But the collapse is being initiated by something else. We need to find out what and then work out how to reverse it."

"How are we supposed to do that?"

"We need to get back another one and a half billion years. There is another hotspot there that I need to analyse. There should be significantly less of these extra bubble universes as well. Without my device, however," she tapped her wrist, "I can't get us anywhere."

"I know where they keep the time capsules," he stated. "In fact, I have already been convicted for stealing one."

If she could not travel using her own devices, she could still use what was available in the simulation.

"Let's go," she demanded.

He tore off down the corridor, deeper into the complex. She followed, still tapping at her dormant device.

Time Capsules were not left lying around for anyone to use. Not only were they held in a secure building, but they were also held within their own bubble universe. It sat on the border of the time vortex, breaching the gap between the dimensions and allowing free and easy access into the time stream. In fact, the vortex itself was all that was required in order to travel through time – anyone could just jump into the open hole and fall anywhere. The Time Capsule was necessary to have any control over the journey.

As Raxus explained these complications to her, she began to question him about how many bubble realities they had created.

"Impossible to say," he shrugged at her. They were now passing through the linking corridor to the Vortex Housing Barracks, where the Capsules were kept. Its looming structure overshadowed the clear, perspex like enclosure they were walking through. Beyond it was a strange, luminescent and sunless sky that created the border of their bubble universe.

"It has been theorized that each bubble universe also has alternate timelines, like the ones running through Universe One."

"Universe One?" she asked, worried about the nomenclature.

"Its our way of delineating our Universe from the others. As we keep interacting with them through paradoxes and the Multiverse War, it helps to be able to keep track of where you came from."

"Multiverse war?" she asked, even more worriedly.

"How do you not know about that?" he asked. "Or the Time War?!"

"Yeah. Time War. That was another thing I wanted to ask you about."

He stared at her – a slow realization dawning across his face.

"You really are not from this universe at all, are you?" he stated, finally. She smiled – pleased that he was catching on.

"In a manner of speaking," she conceded. "There is no Time War nor Multiverse war where I come from."

"Well... the Multiverse War is just a consequence of the Time War," he began to explain – trying not to think too hard about how she came from somewhere that had no experience of either. "As soon as a species reaches the ability to Time Travel, all other species that have developed the ability make stabs at it throughout its timeline. If they survive those initial moments, then they usually hide themselves from the Hybrids and enter negotiations with the rest of us."

"These Hybrids," she interrupted him, "like the spiked cyborg creature that got disintegrated?"

"Yes," he nodded. "They are an inter-universe problem. As they can Time Travel and universe hop, they are spreading throughout the Multiverse. As we are Universe One, at the heart of it all, the other universes declared war on us to try to prevent the Hybrids spreading. They figured that if they rooted out the original seeding ground, then they could prevent the spread."

"I can see the flaw in their logic. If this is the root dimension, then they would cause a major paradox by eliminating it."

"That is the conclusion we all reached after they did it."

"What? Wait... Your universe still exists, right?"

"Yes, but they managed it a few times. Universe One went through a series of catastrophic paradoxes, spontaneously reforming with the other multiverses around the paradox they had caused. Consequently, the other multiverses are either ignorant of their attempt failing or are no longer in a position to war on other universes at all."

"How is it you all know about it?" she asked. "If your universe was the heart of the paradox?"

"We are in a bubble reality here," he explained. "Events that occurred in Universe One no longer affect us. Otherwise the Hybrids would have wiped us out when they destroyed our home world."

"We definitely need to get back there and investigate."

"Do you think that is the paradox that caused the collapse?" he asked, thinking back to his calculation.

"It is not due to paradox," she growled, peevishly. "You need to get that idea out of your head."

"You said yourself you don't understand it!" he objected. "Can't you take the advice of an expert?!"

She slowed and drew his attention towards her eyes, fixing his gaze.

"I am an amalgamated consciousness with several trillion years of experiences. Trust me when I tell you; *I know what I am talking about.* Paradox is having an effect, but it is not the cause of the collapse."

"None of this helps how we are going to get in there," he pointed, indicating the massive, windowless building that was filling the view. They only had a few more dozen yards to travel before they reached the entrance transmat. Without authorization, that would be where their journey ended – stuck at the entrance portal.

"Any ideas?" she asked, hopefully.

"What about that device of yours?" he asked. She shook her head. It was still dormant and gave no indication of what was wrong with it.

"This is your universe, surely you know how to get in there?" she demanded. Now it was his turn to shake his head.

"The transmat beam is programmed to send authorized people. I have not been authorized and you don't even belong in this universe."

Raxus stopped dead in his tracks and stared at the activating transmat. There was a burst of light, a gust of air and suddenly he was standing in front of himself.

"Maybe you should ask him?" Omega asked, wryly.

"Perfect timing," the new him smiled, as if pleased with himself/themselves.

"You can't be here," the original Raxus stated, staring at the dopplegangar. They were breaking a variety of laws of time by doing this.

"You are a copy," the new Raxus explained. "We can jump anywhere we like, now. We are like her. But you will find out about that."

"Where did you come from?" Omega cut in.

"We are from your future. There is a capsule ready and waiting for you in there. I suggest you get a move on – there is not much time."

"Good enough for me," she stated, stepping onto the transmat. Due to the fact that it already recognised her and Raxus (as their older versions had just used the device) it had no problem authorising her for entry. A moment later it was transporting her into another bubble dimension, on the border of the time vortex. Raxus reached out a hand after her but did nothing when she activated the beam and disappeared. His dopplegangar smiled and shook his head.

"Off she goes again. You will get used to that."

"Wait," our Raxus shook his head, still struggling to put aside everything he knew about the laws of time to continue the conversation with himself.

"I know," the older version of himself nodded – as he already knew what he was going to ask. "We are creating a closed time loop around this event. How did we get the capsule originally? - to send it back here to let us in?"

The older Raxus winced, as if trying to suppress the memory that explained the answer.

At that moment the bubble universe instantaneously collapsed and reformed, in an almost invisible wobble. Both versions of him knew what this meant. The collapse was accelerating towards them. They did not have much time.

"Good luck!"

He then pushed himself onto the transmat and the present version of Raxus suddenly appeared next to Omega, within the Vortex Housing Barracks.

Though it appeared as a building on the outside, the need for any form of structure within the bubble universe was redundant. Instead, the entire of space and time seemed to bend in on one point, somewhere on horizon. At the moment, the vortex it bent into just appeared as a swirling dot of ground and sky that spiralled into nothing. What did not help was the way the horizon seemed to shift inwards with it, as if it too was bent inside it. The whole thing gave you the impression of falling down a plug hole, despite the fact that you were not falling at all.

The ground was a smooth marble, which felt like it should slip down towards the vortex. As they stepped forwards, however, they realized the ground did not slope at all and it was reality that sloped inwards, not just the ground and horizon. It was a strange sensation of feeling as if you should be pulled forwards, whilst gravity still acted downwards.

"Is this it?" Omega asked, looking around the desolate, blank landscape and endless stretch of marble floor.

"We should see the capsules as we get closer to the vortex," he nodded, picking up his pace. "We don't have much time. The collapse is starting outside."

She broke into a jog, running a quick calculation in her head to work out roughly how long they had. She did not like the answer she came up with and a second later doubled her pace. After a few moments, six monolithic slabs appeared from the warped horizon. As they got closer, they rapidly grew in size – revealing the strange distortions in perspective caused by the time vortex.

After a few more steps, they suddenly started hearing the strange whine of reality bending. The vortex seemed to shriek its objection at existing. It beckoned her attention, causing her to concentrate on its screaming darkness. It was as if everything wrong with her simulation could be seen within its shifting, falling depths. She didn't even notice her feet slow to a stop – a few feet from one of the monolithic Time Capsules.

Raxus had seen this kind of hypnosis before. It was the kind that could cause lasting insanity if they stared too long. Inside that vortex was literally everything that ever was and could have been. It was the raw code of the universe. He slowed next to her, avoiding the hypnotic depths to concentrate on the monolithic slab before it.

She didn't notice him or the slab any more. Instead, she was focused solely on the swirling depths of existence inside the vortex. There was too much for her mind to process – even with her huge amounts of experience and amalgamated intelligence.

If Omega's device had been working she could have deduced the problem immediately. It would have prevented her needing to gallivant off through the simulation entirely – which is one of the reasons it had stopped working. An explanation for this malfunction will not be forthcoming for some time, however. The frustrations this creates for Omega will become increasingly apparent.

Raxus shoved her into the monolith. She didn't even notice that she fell straight through the strange, obsidian surface. She only snapped back again once she was on the other side, staring into a dormant control chamber. There was a long sofa-like seat around the outside edge, a control desk and six arches bisecting it from the centre. There were no lights on, yet there was still a gentle warm glow in the room – highlighting how bare it actually was.

She stared into the middle distance in a daze, not quite adjusting to where she was.

Raxus had been taught from an early age not to stare too hard at the vortex. It was something that was drilled into every newborn in the bubble, even though most would never see it. An unfortunate few never recovered from their first experience – haunted forever by all the things they could have done. After pushing Omega inside, he made sure he avoided looking into it and turned towards the Capsule.

There were several flashes of light, highlighting his shadow across the obsidian like material of the monolith. He turned around in surprise, wondering why others were following them into the barracks. Then his eyes fell on the distant shape of a galloping Hybrid. Given the shifting perspective caused by the time vortex, he couldn't be sure if it wasn't already on top of him.

He flailed backwards and fell into the capsule, immediately activating the control chamber and sealing the door. Omega jumped and stared at the rapidly lighting chamber. Ignoring her fascination, Raxus lifted his arms and activated the holographic control system over his head. With a few flourishes of his hands, he was preparing to launch the capsule into the vortex.

Launch is probably a little misleading. From the outside it looked more like a flop.

The Hybrid smacked into the sealed capsule in an attempt to follow them. Bouncing off it like a ball, it reeled around and began focusing the millions of needle weapons across its body. At this point, the monolith wobbled, flopped forwards and then dropped into the vortex, leaving the creature behind.

There was no noticeable change within – other than a fluctuation in the readings on Raxus's holographic display. This is what drew Omega's attention and she was soon stepping up next to him so to get a closer look at what he was doing.

"Fascinating," she blinked, still a little overwhelmed by what she had seen in the vortex.

"So you don't travel like this where you come from?" he asked.

"We don't time travel."

There was a short pause after she had made the statement – long enough for him to laugh as if she was joking. He suppressed the chuckle a moment later when he saw she was still being deadly serious.

"I... I don't understand. I saw you time travel earlier... with your device. Didn't I?"

She drew her gaze away from his display and tried to blink away the fuzziness left from the vortex. She failed and instead, she forgot what he had asked. Trying to cover up for this, she then started to make her way to the seat along the edge of the room.

"Are you okay?" he asked, realizing she was still dazed.

"I am processing a lot of information right now," she stated – rationalizing what she had seen. "I just need a moment or two."

"Most people need to sleep it off," he explained.

"Sleep?" she asked, still trying to remember all of the strange things that organics practised. It was getting harder with the splitting headache that was developing in her simulated brain.

"You just stared at the entirety of existence. Not just the universe – every universe that could

possibly be and all of their variations. Most people can't form sentences for weeks."

"I am not most people," was her snippy reply. Again – she wished the device on her wrist still worked. Tapping its dormant screen, she felt her head steadily getting heavier. A slow spin was starting in her vision, drawing her gaze down towards the seat. She slowly lowered her head down onto the soft fabric. It immediately felt better; the cool cushions pressing against her unusually warm temple.

Chapter Four

The Time War

The monolith fell through the vortex like a leaf in a hurricane. Spinning end over end and whipped through the winds of time, it seemed to be flung from one storm into the next without any sign of control. The swirling chaos around it, lit by blue and red flashes, seemed to open into wide yawning gaps of space and stars. Then these holes would suddenly fill, obscured as the vortex convulsed and sent them spinning into a new void.

Raxus remained at the centre of the room, his arms splayed out like a conductor as he tried desperately to control their descent through the timelines. Omega remained sprawled on the seat, trying desperately to get her head to stop throbbing. It was like all of existence and an infinite number of alternative probabilities had opened into her mind. It was too much for even her immense amalgamated intellect.

The monolith shook as they span into the next time stream, jerking her from her daze for a moment. Squinting at the array of holographic controls that Raxus was conducting, she tried to deduce what was happening.

"What is happening?" she asked a moment later, when she realised she had very little understanding of the mechanics of temporal navigation.

"I am trying to get us back through time," he explained, throwing her a glance. "I think the collapse is following us down through the vortex. We keep being shoved into uncontrolled paradoxes."

As he spoke he directed them back away from another yawning chasm of stars that was opening up in front of them. Across the holograms were dozens of others, all highlighted in red to warn him of their approach. Behind them was an increasingly dim spot of darkness, representing the future collapsing and becoming unreachable. At the far end, a long way ahead of them in the vortex, was the ultimate uncontrolled paradox – the Big Bang at the beginning of time.

"Can we get to our destination?" Omega asked, struggling to sit up against the turbulence. The monolith shook once more and suddenly clanged like it had struck something metal. Then it went silent, leaving the echo of the bang reverberating around them. The holographic displays flickered once and then went off, leaving the two of them in an eerie, silent room.

"I think we just crashed," he explained, quietly.

"Where?"

He did not answer immediately and began waving his hands across the central dais, trying to see if anything reacted. When it did not, he sighed and finally responded: "I think *when* might be a more pertinent question."

"How far did we get from the collapse?" Omega asked, rising from the seat to stand next to him. He continued to wave his hands but to no avail.

"Somewhere close to a billion years, I think," he replied, increasingly frustrated with the lack of response from the controls. "Puts us around the year fourteen point eight."

"Good," Omega nodded, confidently calculating the distance from the collapse. "That should give us a few hours before the collapse reaches here."

"No, it is not good," Raxus shook his head, ceasing his flailing arms to face her. "We have been ejected into one of the most uncontrolled paradoxes in history. This entire era is littered with holes into the multiverse and paradox traps. Hybrids and Chronobots and worse hunt the time stream around here. If we get spotted by almost any of the factions in the Time War we are dead. Even our own side will try and stop us for stealing this capsule!"

"So how do we get moving again?" she asked, as if none of the problems he had stated were in the least bit of her concern (which ultimately, they were not).

"I don't know!" he whined back at her. "I am not a time traveller. I am am experimental paradoxologist. My place should be in my laboratory."

"Your laboratory no longer exists," Omega replied, unsympathetically. "By now the collapse would have prevented it from ever existing, along with everyone that you knew. If we do not get going within the next couple of hours, that collapse will reach us here and you will also cease existing along with everything else here."

"I don't know what you want me to do about it?!" Raxus shot back at her, angry that she could so callously describe the end of all existence without a hint of emotion.

"How do we get this thing back into the time stream?" she asked, calmly ignoring his outburst.

"Short of pushing it back into the vortex, I have no idea," he shook his head, growling. "Everything is dead. There is no power going through the controls. It is like the whole thing shorted out when we crashed."

"So we need power?" Omega asked. "What does it run on?"

"It is hooked into the time vortex, using charged tachyons from the local time stream. Areas like this have had their tachyons destroyed by the uncontrolled paradox event. It strands time travellers in areas that have been ripped up in time by other time travellers."

"So there are no tachyons here to power us?"

"Not exactly. There will be Chronobots, Hybrids and who-knows-what-else zipping in and causing the paradox in the first place."

"So we could steal their tachyon energy to power our capsule?" Omega asked, cautiously. Raxus looked at her, worriedly.

"We want to avoid running into any other time travellers, not charge towards them!" he objected. "Our side will take the capsule away again, the Hybrids will kill us on sight and who knows what the Chronobots or others will do!"

"Let me worry about their hostility," Omega waved her hand, confidently. "You just point me in their direction."

"I am not even sure how I am supposed to do that. With no power I can't even tell you where we are."

"Then perhaps we should take a look the old fashioned way?" she suggested, heading for the doorway. Raxus hesitated.

"We have no idea what is on the other side," he stated. "We could literally be anywhere in the universe."

She stepped through without turning back to acknowledge his warning. Wondering if she had a death wish or just thought herself invincible, he muttered his complaints and followed her out.

They emerged from the monolith in a long metal corridor, separated every few feet with massive steel columns. There were huge bulkhead doors that cut the corridor into multiple parts, all of them presently open and the monolith resting against one. Overhead lights dimly lit the area, creating shadows in the recesses of the walls and playing off the piping, cables and wires that weaved through every panel. The entire place felt as if it was only half finished, with large patches missing wall plating or wires and cables jutting out from between unfinished seams. A loud thrum filled the area, echoing up and down the metal pipes that ran along the ceiling.

"Good start," Raxus muttered. "Breathable atmosphere, correct gravity and solid ground beneath our feet."

"You worry too much," Omega stated. "Any idea where we could be, yet?"

"I am going to need a bit more that just a corridor to deduce that," he replied. "Though I would guess we are either on a ship or a space station. The gravity is not quite right – I recognize the spring in it."

"Good. We just need to find our way to a control room, then."

"I imagine they will find us quickly enough," he replied, looking up and down the empty corridor. "Our arrival would have shown. They are not likely to appreciate us turning up like this."

"What is that doing?" Omega asked, stopping to marvel at a bizarre mechanical man in one of the recesses. It was dormant and stared straight ahead through crude, photoreceptive eyes. She could make out parts of its interior workings and the cogs and springs that seemed to run it. None of its parts seemed to be moving.

"That is a Chronobot," Raxus warned her, taking her arm to pull her away from it. "We saw one back in the courtroom."

"What are they?" she asked. Looking over its strange design, she found several things wrong with it – not least that several of the parts appeared to hover around its innards without anything to link them. The whole thing looked like it had been thrown together using clockwork mechanisms and springs.

"They don't look practical," she added.

"They act as guardians to the time lines," he explained, wincing as she lifted a finger to tap it provocatively in the head. "They are supposed to stop paradoxes occurring. Don't do that."

"Paradoxes like us?" she asked, now a little more cautious. Her finger poised over its dormant forehead.

"Potentially," he nodded, relieved that she was being more careful. Confident that it was not going to do anything, she lowered her hand and surveyed the corridor.

"Which way?"

"The power cables lead that way," he pointed to the ceiling. "If we assume they are feeding power from a generator down there..." he pointed downwards, "we can assume that the control room they are feeding is this way!"

* * *

Raxus, being naturally familiar with this universe/simulation, was quite correct in his assumption. A short distance ahead and a few floors above was indeed a control room, currently filled with an assortment of strange creatures who were united in one goal.

The Time War is an unnecessarily complicated consequence of the simulation. It dragged all species capable of time travel into it and immediately tore holes into their history as every species that could ever traverse the vortex attempted to corrupt their temporal streams and stop anyone else from inventing it. At the same time, the descendants of the races that had survived inventing time travel would also be there –

attempting to assure their own futures by stopping other races stopping them and creating more paradoxes. Several species had gone through the inconvenience of both existing and not existing multiple times over.

The war was not going well for this particular group. As a front line outpost, it was sorely lacking in defences against the temporal threats of its enemies. It was an early experimental station in the mechanics of time travel – vital to several species and at the centre of their appearance on the 'time travelling circuit'. In a few short hours they were supposed to test their entry into the time vortex and mark their official entry into the war. Consequently, all other sides involved in the war were adamant in their attempts to prevent them.

"Still nothing from the Celestials," Uthrax barked, as if his report was more important than any of the others. A babble of voices joined his, all calling out equally troubling news from around the system. They were losing on almost every front.

He was an eight foot, eight limb, spinning, jelly-like creature with an array of sensory organs dotted along his arms like spindles. Hailing from a race of similar beings from Andromeda, his people were a vital part of the Supercluster Alliance that led their experiments in time travel. The rest of the control room was filled with other species from three different galaxies, some no more than gaseous particles held together with strings of photons.

"We are losing tachyon stability on the Celestial Guns. They are being removed from the timelines at the point of their creation," the only human-like being reported. Tesla was covered in cybernetic implants and only resembled a man due to his two arms and legs. His head was covered in flashing lights and wires, obscuring his face and hooking him directly into his seat. His people had left Earth a billion years before, altering their DNA and adding to their bodies and brains with more and more mechanical and digital aides. Natural and artificial evolution had pushed them so far from their ancestors that they were no longer regarded as Homo-Sapiens at all.

"Homeworlds report multiple invasions. They are stepping up their assault."

Another voice added – this time translated by changing the colours it emitted into tones that the rest of the room would understand. The myriad of creatures all comprehended it perfectly, but it was the mighty creature in the centre – the commander of the operation, who collated all of the information.

The commander was an Augmented Magua – a huge and bloated creature with six tiny legs to carry it's flea-shaped body. These creatures are of particular note, not just for the grotesque appearance. As the oldest species to have been spawned in the universe, its long civilization had several encounters with the Time War, resulting in several alternative branches of their existence. Their earliest manifestation had been so prejudiced against all other life it had attempted to prevent any other species from ever evolving. The subsequent mess this created will be explored in greater detail later on. At present, it is necessary to be aware that this particular breed of Augmented Magua was now trying to get back into the Time War with the aid of several neighbouring species. This united effort was not without its detractors and several other species, Magua and other time travellers were attempting to stop them.

Its voice vibrated through them like a warm summer's day – working suggestively on their subconsciousness.

They know we are close to completion it's voice boomed through their minds. *We just need to hold them off for a few more hours...*

"We are not going to hold them without help," Uthrax warned. "There is no sign of the Celestials."

They will be back, the commander replied, calmly. *We will hold the line on our own for now.*

"Elders and Hybrids are opening rifts in the heart of Andromeda."

Are they engaging each other or are they attacking our forces?

There was a moment of silence while half a dozen aliens analysed the data streaming in. After a few more seconds of interaction between them, as they debated their findings, Tesla finally answered – collating the information through his multiple augments.

"They are engaging each other. Hybrid forces are moving away. Our forces are being left alone."

Good, the commander soothed. *They will distract one another with their own battles. Hopefully they will distract the Chronobots as well.*

"Unlikely," Tesla replied. "We have paradox events opening up all around us."

That will also help, the commander continued to soothe them all. *We will be masked behind that chaos.*

"Chronobots have been detected in quadrant seven," Uthrax growled, dispelling the calming effect. A wave of fear made its way through the room at their mention. "There is a tachyon hole developing nearby."

Aboard the station? the commander pressed – its telepathic voice soothing despite the concern in its tone.

"Affirmative."

Deploy bots to investigate and suppress the area. We can't afford a breach.

"Scans indicate possible Celestial interference."

Suddenly the atmosphere shifted again, the mention of their saviours' name instilling a new sense of hope in their hopeless situation.

There you go, the commander soothed them. *They have arrived.*

"There are abnormalities in the scan," Tesla warned. "There is another reading showing similar abnormalities and is definitely not a Celestial."

The Magua shifted its huge body around to peer over the cyborg. An array of tiny eyes all squinted down on the much smaller, human-like creature that was wired in below it.

Not a Celestial? it asked, an edge of fear in its telepathic voice. *Then what is it?*

Raxus and Omega stopped suddenly as hatches in the walls opened all around them. A flood of small, cylindrical balls hovered around them in a net, bobbing up and down at head height.

"We surrender," Raxus put his hands up, immediately. "We mean you no harm."

Omega just glared at them and then him, clearly unimpressed with his cowardice.

"Have you worked out which side they are on?" she asked, hoping that his surrender was prompted by something positive.

"No," he shook his head. "But they are not Hybrids. We would be dead already."

"Not bloody likely," was Omega's confident response. Turning authoritatively to one of the floating balls, she leaned in close to it.

"Take me to your leader," she demanded. The ball seemed to ignore her, hovering in front of her face. Raxus just winced.

"I think they are meant to hold us here until they can send someone," he explained. "My people used similar things way back in the dawn of our civilization. They are not very complicated."

Omega tapped the floating ball provocatively, causing Raxus to scowl and step away. The ball sparked slightly but made no further aggressive moves. She shrugged and pushed past it.

"Wait!" Raxus objected, worriedly waving his arms as half of the balls swarmed around her. All of them began sparking. Omega ignored them and continued down the corridor.

"You said it was this way?" she asked, swatting one that floated too close. They sparked a little more aggressively but stayed out of reach. Raxus hesitated, staring at the collection hovering around him.

"I think so..." was his less confident reply. Taking a step forward, he winced as they sparked. The flickers of current seemed to lick out towards him but did no damage. He took another, more confident step forwards.

"Hurry up," she called back to him, still ignoring the sparking balls as they swarmed angrily around her. He put his head down and ignored them, making his way along the corridor behind her.

"Neither targets are reacting to the energy barriers. We are cycling emissions to attempt to identify their shielding."

The commander was now linked directly into the bots and was staring at the data with increasing concern.

They both looked like Celestials – mimicking a human form that more closely resembled Homo-Sapiens than the cyborg; Tesla. But the scans told a different story – especially for the female looking one.

Can we get anything clearer on her? he asked, directing Tesla to focus the balls' attentions on Omega.

"That is the best we can get. She does not appear to be made from any kind of recognizable form of matter. She could be an advanced photon projection. Possibly a Hard Light Drive."

And what about him? the Magua asked, focusing now on Raxus.

"He could be made of something similar, but we are showing him as a recognized Celestial."

"One Celestial will not be much help," Uthrax commented. "We are losing the Outer Sectors."

The commander ignored the spinning jelly-like being and focused on their two intruders, now almost directly below them.

What is he doing with her and where are all the other Celestials?

"We have another internal tachyon emission localising in their area," Tesla warned. A red glow appeared on his holographic map where he indicated, showing the location.

Is the Chronobot reacting to it?

"Negative. It is still dormant."

That is good news at least. Is it one of ours?

"Tachyon emissions indicate that it is a localised leap. It looks unstable."

Estimated era?

"Within a hundred years," Tesla reported back – calculating immense numbers through his augments. "Its not clear if they have jumped back or forward, but the emissions match early Celestial capabilities."

"It appears to be heading off to intercept our two unknown guests," Uthrax commented. "Maybe it is going to deal with them?"

Hopefully we will get some answers. Keep your attention on the external assault. Notify me if that Chronobot wakes up.

The control room returned to its hub of activity, the huge Magua in its centre shifting its weight nervously to watch Tesla's display. They were losing territory all around the system, pressed in on every side by near infinite numbers of enemies.

Its uneasiness emanated around it like a bad smell, affecting every one of its subordinates and affirming them with an even greater determination.

"Stop where you are."

Omega sighed, hearing the voice and the supposed authority that it was delivered with. If she had not lost the use of her bracelet, none of this would have been a problem and she wouldn't need to turn around. Without it, she had no choice but to find out why this person thought they had any authority over her.

"Who are you?" she growled, turning to look over the figure that had addressed them. Raxus did the same, raising his hands as he did so. He immediately recognised the officer standing in front of him. He also knew how awkward any explanation he gave would be.

"You need to answer my questions first," the officer demanded. He was dressed in a tight fitting black tunic and appeared to be human – in the same manner that Raxus was. He was holding a cylindrical device out towards them as if it was a weapon and waved it threateningly as he spoke. Omega ignored it.

"You haven't asked any questions," she stated, obtusely. "I have. Answer it."

"You are trespassing in a region of temporal instability," he responded, shifting the device towards Raxus (who raised his hands a little higher). "Your era signed a treaty stating that you would not interfere. What are you doing here?"

"It is an accident. We crashed. We didn't intend to stop here," Raxus blurted out, looking terrified as the barrel of his device was aimed into his face. "*Please* don't eradicate us."

Omega sighed again and placed her hand on the barrel, forcing it away from Raxus.

"Stop threatening my friend," she growled, as the weapon turned towards her again. "We are not here to do any harm. Quite the opposite, in fact."

"You need to tell me who you are," he demanded, stepping back so the weapon was no longer in her grasp. Taking hold of the cylinder with both hands, he levelled it at her to make it quite clear he wanted an immediate answer.

"The future is collapsing," Raxus blurted out again, his hands still high in the air. This caused both of them to shift their attention to him. Omega folded her arms angrily, wondering how he was going to explain it. The officer shifted his attention to him with growing panic.

"What do you know of that?" he demanded, stepping forwards again. Omega immediately took hold of the barrel, shifting it away from both Raxus and herself. This time he fired, letting a bolt of energy materialize against the wall that it was pointed towards. That metal panels dissolved, leaving Omega to look down in surprise and horror at what the weapon was capable of.

"Give me that thing!" she demanded, snatching it out of his grip. The officer backed off, holding his hands up. Raxus looked between her and him and slowly lowered his own.

"What are you doing here and who are you?" Omega asked, lazily waving the device towards the officer. He kept his hands up.

"I was patrolling the early era when the Celestials disappeared. I picked up your tachyon trace and figured you must have something to do with it. Then we lost contact with other Time Agents – ones closer to my own era."

"Yes, yes. Time is collapsing," she sighed. "We have no more than a few hours before the shock wave reaches here. You will have even less time before it hits your home era and you disappear from existence entirely."

"How do you know this?" he demanded, before realizing he no longer had the weapon. She answered, despite this.

"We are from the year sixteen billion. We fled the collapse."

"If you are from a future that no longer exists..." he began, lowering his arms, "how do you still exist?"

"I am still trying to get my head around that," Raxus commented, quietly.

"We are unique," Omega smiled. "You need to worry about what you will do before your era disappears."

"Never mind that," the officer growled. "If this era disappears it means we will never develop time travel at all. If that happens there will be paradoxes echoing all the way back through time."

"Time is already collapsing," Omega sighed. "The paradox effects you keep talking about will pall in comparison to it not existing in the first place."

"No, he is right," Raxus insisted. "This is my speciality. If we lose this era then earlier eras will be jeopardised by the paradox. There will be instantaneous collapses in reality, based around the moments when later eras interfered."

"You are talking nonsense at me," Omega sighed. "I don't deal with paradoxes."

"Each decision creates alternate realities where every possibility is played out through the infinite," Raxus hurriedly began explaining – using his fingers to try and represent each path of time. "Where we bend time back to make the same decision again," he bent his forefinger round to make the point, "we create further realities that are meshed with the original one," his other hand came up now to add further branches from where his finger bent back. "The time line becomes an increasingly complicated weave of paradoxical causalities, linking back to each main event."

"The point, Raxus?" she asked, looking unimpressed at his now tangled fingers.

"The multiverse will start breaking down – all possible realities will start falling in on this moment."

"All of your reality is collapsing," she sighed. "I am sure I made that clear to you."

Raxus focussed mainly on the 'your' part of the sentence and the tone with which it was delivered. She had already told him that she was not local, but he had assumed that she was from some other part of the multiverse. Now he was starting to wonder what kind of 'reality' she might be from.

"All of reality?" the officer asked, focussing on her words, instead.

"Everything," Omega confirmed. She handed his weapon back to him – seeing how crestfallen her answer had made him.

"I need to get back to my capsule," he whispered, taking the device.

"Can you power ours?" Raxus asked, hopefully. He was met with a dejected shake of the head.

"It was drained when I came into this era – the same as you. All we can do is wait for the temporal fluctuations from the Hybrid assault and ride their shock wave out."

"I doubt you have that much time," she smiled sadly at him. He frowned at her and blinked out of existence. Raxus stared at the spot that he had occupied, mouth agape.

"Did he just?..."

"His era just stopped existing," Omega nodded, showing little sympathy. "We probably have not got much time left."

Chapter Five

The Multiverse War

Omega reached the lift shaft and stared up into its heights. The tube seemed to go for miles in either direction, but upon closer inspection was actually warped in space. What should have only been a few feet twisted so that it appeared several dozen meters distant. It was slightly disconcerting, making her feel smaller the further into the distance she looked. She was trying to guess how much of a warp was involved when Raxus stepped into it. A moment later his body was stretching and disappearing – transported to the next level in the blink of an eye.

Omega followed him through and emerged into the control room, confronted by the myriad of species that occupied it. It took her a moment to process all of the different aliens within the room, many of which had been extinct before her people had amalgamated their consciousnesses. She had programmed their existence into the simulation, using the available knowledge of the past to make them as realistic as possible. Confronted with the feat of her creation, she was slightly in awe of the variety of life that the universe had spawned. And this was just a dozen examples from a trio of galaxies in one single supercluster.

What are you and what do you want? the Magua demanded, its telepathic voice oddly soothing. Omega smiled, overwhelmed by the fact that she had just felt a Magua speak.

"I am from the future," Raxus explained, holding his hands up. "We need your help to get back into the time vortex."

Where are the other Celestials? the huge creature demanded, shifting its attention over him. Omega continued smirking to herself; marvelling at the alien being. The Magua were the eldest known species in her universe – long extinct in her time (along with every other species, effectively). She had always imagined seeing one in the 'flesh' when the simulation was completed – an opportunity to see the very first forms of life that walked the universe. It was only now as she faced the creature that she remembered why her simulation was so important to her.

"Celestials?" Raxus asked, slightly confused by the question. "Oh," he realised - "you mean my people?"

We need your help! All of the other Celestials disappeared!

"We can't hold the line," Tesla added. "They are pushing through."

"I can't help," Raxus objected, holding his hands up apologetically. "I am not from *that* future. We have a truce..."

A truce? the Commander demanded. The Time War was a confusing and often contradictory event. The truce he referred to only existed to prevent them wiping each other out and destroying the universe. Now that the universe was collapsing on its own, the reasons for that truce were largely redundant – a fact that Omega pointed out to Raxus (loudly and in front of all of the aliens in the room).

And who is this with you? the Magua asked, pointing one of its spindly limbs in her direction. *She is not a Celestial. We are not sure what she is.*

"She is travelling with me. As I said, we just need to get out of your way. We are not involved in this war."

"Sector six has fallen. We are losing temporal shielding."

The report only served to agitate the commander further, causing it to bare down on Raxus.

Where are the other Celestials?! it asked again, increasingly frantic.

"I don't know," Raxus shook his head. "If they said they would be here, they will be here."

"No they will not," Omega shook her head. "Think about it: The future is collapsing. There is nobody left to help any more. That agent was probably one of the last."

Raxus did think about it and then suddenly went pale. His own time was now long collapsed – the area of the future his people were from no longer existed. That echo was going all the way down through time, wiping them out from the year sixteen billion, back towards the 'present' (the moment in time they were currently occupying). No help would come as the future it was coming from no longer existed. Which meant they were about to lose the Time War in a spectacular fashion.

"We need to get out of here," he muttered, sinking down next to the giant Magua Commander.

The sight of a 'Celestial' falling to his knees in terror was enough to send a wave of panic through the control room. A flurry of updates and reports were suddenly voiced at the commander as the middle system defences started to fall. Their enemies were closing in all around them.

The future is collapsing? the Magua asked, it's telepathic echo quietening. *What about the Celestials?*

"There are no more Celestials," Raxus shook his head. "We just lost the Time War."

"To be fair," Omega interrupted. "I don't think anyone is going to win this particular conflict. Your universe is collapsing."

What are you? it asked her again, hefting itself between her and Raxus. She marvelled at the beast, slightly awestruck – which was exactly the response she had expected when she had programmed the elder aliens into the simulation.

She ignored the question and patted its muscular, fleshy side.

"You are quite amazing," she smiled. Stepping around it, she found Raxus, still kneeling on the floor. Indicating to the the screens before Tesla and Uthrax, she tried to draw his attention to them.

"If I am reading this right, the borders of this system are rife with tachyon energy," she stated, marvelling at the various screens.

Raxus looked up and followed her gaze around the room, realizing that she was correct. The control room was largely set up to detect and manipulate tachyons. Evidence of it was everywhere around him. Central to all of this were the Hybrid invasion fleets, creating huge waves of energy around them as they pushed in through the system defences. If they could get access to that power their capsule would charge almost immediately. Unfortunately that either required them to be in the centre of the invasion fleet or for the invasion fleet to centre over them. He was not attracted by either concept. He quickly explained this to Omega, who folded her arms.

"I guess we wait for them to come to us," she stated. "By the looks of it they will be on the station in minutes."

And you will do nothing to help us? the Magua demanded, wondering why she was being so callous about their imminent destruction.

"We are not part of the war," Raxus insisted. "We should not even be here."

But if we fail here, your time-line will no longer exist! the Magua continued, its soothing voice now becoming grating and frantic. *The fate of the universe depends on us!*

"They are at the entrance hatches," Uthrax reported. "We have breaches opening all over the station."

"The temporal shields are collapsing. We are picking up multiple rifts forming in the vortex."

It is over, the Magua whispered.

The station hung in deep space, far from any inhabited system or star. All around it were blossoming eruptions and surges of energy. Tiny weapons emplacements, hidden in the darkness, lanced beams of plasma and power, picking at the swarms of Hybrids that swamped the edges of the system. Tiny flashes picked out where they hit one, as the cybernetic creatures exploded spectacularly. It did nothing to slow their approach. The endless wave of these creatures moved like a storm front, bubbling up like a black cloud before descending and ripping everything apart. Their tiny limbs disassembled the weapons and reconstituted their parts into their own bodies – growing as they surged forward.

Then something extraordinary happened. As the Hybrids smashed their way onto the station, rifts began opening all across space. They flickered to start with, like tiny new stars twinkling in the darkness. Then they grew, tearing like rips, blossoming deadly radiation and light as they unzipped existence like a cheap dress. From these holes in reality swarmed all types of craft and creatures, as if all of hell had just opened up above their heads. An array of colours and light followed them through, blanketing space with strange flickers of energy that did not belong in this universe.

Within the room, it was displayed across the projections as sudden shifts in data. Where a steady stream of digits or gentle wave functions had dominated them, they were now asunder with warped readings and random numbers. All of the analysts were alive with activity, trying to understand the information being disseminated.

Outside, the view was quite different. Great lances of energy were being thrown from the rifts and a variety of ships, creatures and monstrosities were emerging from them. The Hybrids that had been swarming up to their station were now in chaos, caught between their dwindling defences and the forces from the rifts.

What is happening? the Magua demanded. A babble of responses failed to explain it and it raised a spindly leg to cease the barrage. Raxus rose and began staring into the readouts – recognising the temporal fluctuations in a way that they could not.

"Come on," Omega insisted, placing a hand on his back. "We need to be at the capsule when they arrive."

He raised his hand to stop her, stepping up next to the Magua Commander.

"They are dimensional rifts," he explained. "Those are invaders from other universes – other time lines."

More attackers? the Magua asked, watching the near infinite numbers pouring through the rifts. They were already overwhelmed.

"We are receiving a message," Tesla stated, mechanically turning towards his commander. "I am relaying it with translation:

"We have traced the collapse to your time-line. We have confirmed that your universe is the epicentre of the destruction that is unravelling our reality. Prepare to receive temporal assistance to maintain your timeline."

"They are here to help?" Raxus asked, looking at Omega. She just frowned and shrugged.

"I figure that the collapse of your reality is not in their best interest, either," was her nonchalant reply. "Its largely irrelevant to us. Any solution they might have is going to be temporary at best."

"How can you be so sure?"

"Because existence should not be collapsing at all. We do not have much time before it reverberates here."

"You said we had hours?!"

"I guessed. I am not willing to hang around to see how accurate that guess was. It is not as if there is a simple formula to work this out."

"We are receiving more surges in tachyons," Tesla warned. "Chronobots are attacking the rifts."

"Chronobots?!" Raxus exclaimed. Omega now pulled him physically towards the lift while he scanned the room.

Stay out of their way, the Magua ordered. *Get our defences back up and clear the Hybrids from the hatches.*

"It's chaos out there," Uthrax wheezed. "The rift invaders are turning on each other. Their Hybrids appear to be joining with ours. The Chronobots are... they are taking out our defences! They are not engaging the Hybrids at all!"

"We need to go," Omega insisted, sharing her gaze between the chaos being displayed and Raxus, who was transfixed. He thought he had understood what was going on for a moment. Now everything was chaos again. Outside, the battle seemed to be a free-for-all, as all sides now seemed to be attacking each other.

Hauling Raxus to the lift tube, Omega shoved him inside while he continued to stare. None of it made any sense to her – most of the creatures and civilizations battling out there either never existed in her universe or had died out aeons before. There was certainly nothing like the Multiverse War in the 'real world'.

Giant warships from far flung universes were torn apart by Hybrid monstrosities made from semi-organic beasts. Tiny, clockwork Chronobots swam between them, removing random beings from the timeline – preventing their paradoxes by deleting them from existence.

Omega pushed Raxus down the corridor they had started in, hoping that they would reach the Capsule before the collapse reached them. Raxus was more worried about the fleets of invaders just outside. Reverberations echoed through the station as dozens of hatchways were forced or blasted open. The lights flickered, dropping them momentarily into darkness. The shadows that appeared with the lights seemed longer than before.

By the time they got back into the capsule, the device had gorged on the horde of tachyons that had been injected into the area. Not waiting to see what happened to the station, Raxus immediately dropped them back into the vortex. The monolith wobbled once and then seemed to flop through the floor, disappearing from the station and dropping through time like a stone.

Chapter Six

The Battle For Aisle Six

Somewhere in an insignificant corner of the Laniakea Supercluster was a small collection of about a hundred galaxies known as the Virgo supercluster. Deep inside this and spiralling around with a much larger galaxy was the Milky Way. Following one of the smaller branches off the Orion Arm, we come to an insignificant, normal looking star and eight planets. One of those planets, hanging in the optimum distance from its sun, was called the Earth.

It was at the height of the Covid19 lockdown, with coronafear rampant throughout the planet.

Prime Ministers and Presidents had caught the virus, affecting the already galloping paranoia. Keyboard warriors dominated social media, infecting the rest of the public with their madness. Traditional media outlets struggled to make news of the reoccurring tragedy as death tolls mounted across the world. All the time, outside, the gentle breeze and chirping birds of early Spring seemed in complete contrast to the turmoil within. Gentle jazz drifted from between open windows and replaced the usual rumble of traffic and aeroplanes. It was like every day had become a lazy Sunday – reminiscent of childhood peacefulness.

Nobody noticed the monolith appearing out of nowhere on the corner of Ivy Street. It wobbled slightly and then rested gently upright, a few inches from the wall of the house on the corner. A few seconds later, Harmony rounded that corner and walked straight past it, giving it almost no attention as she hurried her shopping back into her house.

Dropping two bags of groceries through the door, she turned to close it and spotted the monolith out of the corner of her eye. She paused for a half second – the door hesitating in her hand. Then she pushed it shut and pushed it out of her mind. She had far more pressing concerns at that moment – most of which were focused around the groceries at her feet.

Moving everything to the kitchen, she winced as she heard the radio playing the news jingle. She had left the device on when she had left the house, leaving the dull tones of the newscaster to haunt the air. It helped to discourage opportunist thieves – which she was now convinced patrolled the quiet streets while everyone was locked inside. The newscaster did nothing to allay that fear and after a few moments she turned it off. She had heard enough dedications to the dying Prime Minister and his legacy. They seemed to be ignoring the fact that he was also the same Prime Minister that had destroyed their economy, cut off their trade with Europe and lost the huge science grant that came with it.

This last point was what had rattled her the most – and was largely why she could find little sympathy for him now.

She had been part of a British research team based near Geneva at the Large Hadron Collider. When the British venture into Europe ended, so did their research grant and their unimpaired access to the largest piece of scientific equipment in the world. Her research had been halted, her funds suspended and a flight booked for her back to the United Kingdom. As she had watched the beauty of Lake Geneva recede from her window, she'd still believed she might yet come back again. She still hoped that it all might come undone and she would be allowed to work with her European comrades once more.

That was before the virus had spread.

She was grateful she lived alone. Not only did she fear the risk of having someone else in the house to catch the virus from, but she also despised most other people. She was more than happy like this. She was amply capable of keeping herself occupied – despite being unemployed and locked down during a pandemic. She built graphs of the spreading virus, wrote a new introduction to her thesis and sent off almost a dozen research grant applications. She painted the rear balcony to her room and re-varnished the decking. She baked herself a huge cake and then spent a single evening devouring it on the sofa, in front of an endless run of Netflix.

Days had started to blend into one another. The continually pleasant weather, the gentle sunshine and breezes all contributed to the sameness. On days when she had a siesta halfway through the afternoon, she found the passage of time all the more confusing.

That was until today.

The first thing to trigger her was the lack of coffee in her cupboard. In her half awake state she had failed to think about the fact that she had run out and instead spent ten minutes tearing apart all of the cupboards in an attempt to find the beans. She even checked the fridge – as it would not have been the first time she had absent mindedly put it in there (and the milk in the cupboard).

After searching everywhere possible, her brain woke up enough to remind her that she had run out of beans yesterday afternoon. This drained her of all energy and left her slumped down on the floor, resting her back against the cupboard they should have been in.

It took another hour for her to get dressed and make herself feel at least partially capable of facing the world. A swift cup of tea invigorated her enough to put shoes on and then she was venturing out into the near-apocalyptic streets of East London.

The warm sun, cloudless sky and gentle chirrup of the birds completely contrasted her feeling of imminent doom. The fear that grew inside evaporated as she emerged into the sunshine. There was a literal breath of fresh air – washing away the stagnant smells that had accumulated around her.

Her first steps were still cautious, as if she feared seeing anyone else outside. The other houses on her street were closed up and silent, with only an occasional flicker from someone within or a television refracting on the window. Nobody else was on the street, giving her the confidence to push on. She didn't see another soul until she reached the main road. She stopped for a moment at the corner, watching the other pedestrians march up and down it. There was a car every few seconds and dozens of people – keeping in pairs and avoiding one another like they all had the plague.

She stepped out onto the street, keeping her distance from everyone and lifting her mask over her face.

The shop had a queue outside, with each person standing two meters from the next over crude, blue, foot shaped markings on the floor. She joined the back of these and stared past the four others ahead of her, at the security guard who grimly stood at the door.

One of the people ahead of her coughed. She looked terrified and then apologetic as everyone around her shuffled away. Harmony grimaced and took out her phone, absent mindedly swiping the unlock. It immediately flashed up a host of alerts, drawing her to check on her Twitter account while passing the time in the queue.

Whilst working in Geneva, she had created a profile called 'Higg Higg Hooray' – largely to promote her work at CERN. Since leaving she had continued to maintain it, replying to any professional queries or physics students that were interested. Most of her time, however, was spent browsing and deleting the ignorant comments by the general public that highlighted the lack of understanding of quantum physics. Today was no different and after scowling at the first few comments, she hovered over the fifth one down:

Tetraquarks and Bosons from Twits and Bozos. What is this good for? It is hardly going to make my car faster or toaster cheaper. Science used to be useful. Now it is just silly.

She deleted the comment and continued to search for a genuine query.

She failed.

She spent twenty minutes waiting to get into the shop. When she finally reached the door, she grabbed a basket and immediately headed for the coffee section, hesitating to pick up a few extra pieces that she needed. Chocolate did not necessarily fall into the 'need' category, but the Swiss brand that they had stocked reminded her of her old job. She could not resist picking up a bar.

This delayed her by a few seconds and she reached the coffee aisle just as the woman who had been coughing took the last bag of beans.

Harmony stared in horror at the empty shelf, desperately scanning over it in the hope that she would spot a hidden bag. The row above had grounded coffee and the row below had freeze dried, but there was nothing in the beans section.

A rational way to react would be to either make do with one of the others or try a different shop. Without her morning coffee, however, Harmony was not about to start thinking rationally. Instead, her first reaction was to pull all of the grounded coffee off the shelf in the hope that one of them was actually a bag of beans.

This did not take long.

Shoving the bags haphazardly back onto the shelf and ignoring the condescending tut from an older lady who was watching, she stumbled down the aisle and into the next one.

She heard her cough before she spotted her. The other shoppers all shifted away from her, creating an area around her that they believed would be safe. The woman that was coughing apologised again and looked awkwardly at the other patrons – all of whom were now glaring at her as if she had just sentenced them to death.

Harmony did not, however. She focussed on the bag of Swiss coffee beans poking out of her trolley like it was taunting her.

She moved down the aisle like a cat, prowling after her prey while the rest of the patrons started shuffling away. The coughing woman moved the trolley further along, only to stop again to pick through a variety of yoghurt.

Harmony hesitated next to the cheese, pretending to examine them before picking the one she always bought. The coughing woman put a double pack of yoghurt on top of the bag of coffee beans and moved away. Harmony moved in for the kill.

Dropping the cheese into her basket, she accelerated her pace suddenly and came up behind the coughing woman. Moving in close next to her, she then overtook her and moved up alongside her trolley. A heartbeat later, her eyes were flicking to the yoghurt and coffee beans below them.

Another heartbeat had her considering what she was about to do. It was petty, it felt like stealing and it was mean to the woman she was planning to take the beans from.

She needed that coffee. It wasn't stealing as she hadn't paid for it. The woman should not be shopping if she was coughing and spreading coronavirus to everyone.

She justified it within another heartbeat and found her hand almost unconsciously reaching out to fulfil her desire.

She faked a stumble, put her hand out to knock the yoghurt away and then wrapped her fingers around the coffee – pretending that she was using it to support her weight.

The fake stumble was not fooling anyone and when she withdrew her hand (the coffee clearly clasped in her fingers), the coughing woman almost immediately reacted.

"What do you think you are doing?!" she shrieked, pulling her trolley away from her.

Harmony looked at her, then the coffee beans and then back at her.

The woman started to cough again, lifting one hand to cover her mouth. The rest of the patrons backed away again. Harmony thought about answering and then realised this was the perfect opportunity to just walk away.

She turned and marched back up the aisle, leaving the coughing woman spluttering her objections as everyone else scowled and avoided her. Hauling her trolley around with one hand, she shouted after Harmony, finally getting a hold of her cough.

Turning into the next aisle, Harmony thought she had given the woman the slip. She could not hear her coughing and there was no sign of her trolley following her. Shoving the beans into her basket, she confidently marched towards the checkout.

The trolley was launched into her ankles just as she reached the corner of aisle six. It was not hard enough to push her over, but was definitely delivered with enough force to bruise her ankle. Harmony yelped, swung round and almost threw the contents of her basket all over the shop.

"Give my coffee beans back," the woman demanded from behind her trolley.

"I beg your pardon?!" Harmony objected, feigning complete innocence.

"We all saw you. You took my damn beans. Give them back."

"Beans?" she asked, wide-eyed and trying her best to look as stupid and innocent as possible.

"The damn coffee beans! There! In your basket!"

Harmony put a hand over her basket, as if covering it would help disguise the fact that the beans were there. It did not work, but the woman was too busy coughing again to follow up on the point.

"Is there a problem here?" the security guard asked, lumbering up to them. There was a line of angry looking patrons staring at them from the doorway and more trying to navigate around them without breaching social distancing. They appeared to be creating a crowd.

"She stole my coffee beans," the coughing woman finally managed to get out, croaking slightly. The security guard winced at her and then turned to Harmony.

"Is this true?"

"Of course not," she snapped back, removing the beans from the basket. "They have not been paid for yet. I just picked them up."

"The last damn packet!" the coughing woman interrupted. "She stole it out of my trolley."

"Did you?" the security guard asked, turning back to Harmony.

"Of course not! There are plenty of packets on the shelf. Why would I take it from her?!"

The security guard sighed and looked back at the other woman again.

"Have you tried taking another bag?" he asked.

"That was the last one!"

"Have you checked?"

"Well... no..." the coughing woman stuttered. "She took it from my trolley!"

Harmony smiled sweetly at the security guard – confident that she had won him over.

"Why don't you come with me and check for another one?" he asked the coughing woman, patronisingly. She glared at both of them and then swung the trolley back around again – doing her best to try and graze Harmony as she swung it. She failed and with an angry growl from the back of her throat, she marched back up the aisle and towards the coffee again.

"Thank you," Harmony smiled at the guard, making her way to the checkout. Using the self service one, she got out of the shop again as quickly as possible – hoping to avoid another confrontation with the coughing woman. For one thing – she really did not want to catch whatever it was that gave her the cough.

This was by far the most straight forward encounter that Harmony would experience that day.

Her day was about to get a lot more strange. It began again a few minutes after she got home and just after she ignored the strange monolith on the corner of her street. It started with a knock on her door and an identically dressed man and woman on her doorstep.

It started with Omega asking this one simple, innocuous question:

"Have you noticed anything that could indicate the end of the world?"

Chapter Seven

The Swiss Coffee

Harmony stared at the woman as if she was a stain on her dress, or sputum waiting to be wiped away.

They were standing on her doorstep, staring up at her in matching uniforms, waiting for her to answer.

"Are you serious?" she asked, finally.

"Quite," Omega responded, deadly serious. Raxus just looked apologetically to one side, as if he wasn't keen on getting involved. Neither of them realized the ridiculousness of their situation or the question.

"End of the world?" Harmony countered, drily. "Like the virus?"

"Virus?" Omega frowned. "No, nothing like that."

"You aren't serious," Harmony decided, moving to close the door. She didn't like them that close to her – breathing on her from her doorstep. Her paranoia was strong enough to make her wonder what they were doing out in the first place.

"Do you mind if we come in?" Omega asked, pushing forwards before she could close it. More afraid of being breathed on with a virus breath, Harmony shrunk back from the door and looked worriedly at them as Omega pushed her way inside. She had surprising strength.

"Its just a few questions," she insisted, holding her hand up apologetically. Harmony considered screaming and calling for the police. There was something about the way Omega had said it, combined with the alluring beauty of her features, that made her believe her. She found herself thinking that they did not look like criminals – both of them seemed to have an intelligence and beauty that implied that they never needed to break the law. Then there was their strange, matching uniforms.

"Questions?..." she asked, hesitantly. "What questions? Who are you?"

"I am Omega. This is my colleague; Raxus. We need to ask some important questions."

Their names sounded official and possibly coded, like secret agents. This just doubled her already heightened paranoia.

"I have only been out for shopping," she blurted out – as if she was worried about what they had seen her doing.

"Shopping?" Raxus asked, completely at a loss as to what she meant.

"My groceries. Food. Only essentials. It is allowed."

Her short, truncated sentences did not ease the confusion between them. Omega stepped in again, taking control of the conversation.

"We need to know if you have noticed anything unusual," she continued.

Harmony finally shook off the paranoia and tried again to ascertain who these people were. Were they now expecting her to start grassing on her neighbours? Or snooping on who was outside when they shouldn't?

"Unusual?" she asked, wondering why secret agents would wear obvious and matching uniforms.

"Yes. Things that appear out of place."

"There is a large black slab that has appeared on the corner," she indicated out of the door. "That wasn't there this morning."

Both of them looked nervously across at each other. They did not elaborate and Omega continued her questioning.

"Any other strange things appearing or disappearing? Loss of time or sudden changes in what you thought was normal life?"

"What do you mean by 'normal life'?" was the dry response.

Omega tried thinking of a specific failure in physics and gravity that could indicate the simulation shutting down/universe collapsing.

"Things dropping at different speeds to what they normally do?" she asked, raising and lowering her hand as if to demonstrate. Harmony stared at her as if she was mad – which she was rapidly concluding.

"Like gravity?" she asked.

"Yes!" Omega beamed, as if she had been unsure that Harmony would understand the concept. "A localized failure in gravity waves coalescing in subspace? Or perhaps an inexplicable fluctuation in photon interference patterns?"

The last statement confirmed it. She was clearly mad and spouting rubbish from science fiction. The sheepish looking man was either her (massively inefficient) carer or a fellow loon, helping her spread her madness.

"I think you need to go," she suggested, turning towards Raxus. "Both of you..."

"Can you answer the question?" Omega insisted. Harmony shook her head and with some struggle turned her gaze back towards her.

"No. Gravity has been behaving just fine. Other than you and that slab outside, my day had been fairly normal."

"Good," Omega affirmed – leaving Harmony even more exasperated. At least if she had shown that she had been expecting some kind of ridiculous failure in reality it would have affirmed how mad she was. The fact that she was reassured by it not happening just annoyed her further.

"Are you leaving now?" she asked, pointing at her door.

"No," Omega shook her head, decisively. "There is something that is causing a rip. We need to find out what, where and why."

"Right," Harmony sighed. That confirmed it. "Before the end of the world. You mentioned that."

"And you are sure you have had no indication of it ending?" Raxus asked, feeling that the woman was intelligent. He was also interested about the virus she had mentioned – despite it not having any clear relevance to the end of the universe as a whole.

"Other than several hundred thousand dead of a flu virus," she growled. "We also have global warming, nuclear weapons and idiot leaders."

"This flu virus," Raxus stepped towards her. "How contagious is it?"

"Very," she replied, stepping away. "Which is why you shouldn't be just walking into people's houses and spreading it."

"I apologize," he held up a hand. "We do not mean to alarm. Let me assure you that we certainly do not carry this virus."

"Right," she nodded, sarcastically. "I guess its too late now, if you did."

Omega was ignoring them both and looking around the entrance hall of her home and investigating the pictures on the wall. She seemed to be sniffing the air, as if searching for something. It just annoyed Harmony further – making her think that she was offended by the aroma she had built up while in lockdown.

"Have there been any inconsistencies about the virus?" he asked, keeping his distance. "Have the numbers of deaths been fluctuating unusually?"

"Good question," Omega agreed, turning from the walls. "Has anyone come back to life from it?"

Harmony sighed and did her best to ignore the other woman and responded to Raxus, instead. He seemed at least partially sane.

"The figures in the media are always contradicting themselves," she shrugged. "But they always do that – whether it's economics, viruses or homicides. It depends which source you use."

"How much do these media disagree? Can you show an example?"

"You just need to Google it. A quick search will find you six different figures for yesterday's deaths."

"Do you mind?" he asked, indicating that he would very much like to see. She shrugged and led them out of the hall and through to the kitchen. Omega stopped as she passed the half empty shopping bag. She dropped to one knee and put her hand in the bag, ignoring the other two as they continued into Harmony's study.

She kept a clean room for her work, even though she had been unemployed for some time. There were study books neatly arranged around the screen and the keyboard was left waiting on her desk. The walls were covered in a variety of pictures, awards, certificates and book shelves. The room was small, but seemed even smaller with everything in there.

It took a few moments for the computer to boot up, much to Raxus's wry amusement. In his era, the waiting time for a computer to boot was measured in fractions of nanoseconds. He was confused when the screen didn't immediately light, worried when it showed some kind of boot screen and then disappointed when it took almost half a minute to finally get to the Windows login.

"Can you look away for a moment?" she asked, leaning over the keyboard. She was awkwardly aware of how close he was and how easily he could see her enter her password.

He had no idea, however, and simply obliged while smiling like a moron. When she finished, he turned back round with the same expression. It then took her a further half minute to get Chrome loaded and then Google the day's death statistics.

"What is that?" he asked, leaning over her as she started clicking her way through the search results. He was fascinated by a pop up on the top right corner, advertising an AI chatbot by something called MobiMonkey.

"Its an advert," she growled at him, avoiding the tiny advert. "I can't get rid of the damn thing. I think I downloaded a virus with it at some point."

"You download the virus?" he asked, incredulous and slightly confused about their level of technology. In his era the idea that you could download a virus was horrifying – being that their entire culture was backed up in digital formats and deposited into an organic body each day. If Omega had been present for the conversation it may have conjured even more fears, as her reality was entirely digital.

"No," Harmony sighed. "Its a computer virus. Not a human virus. I probably clicked on something I shouldn't have."

"Clicked?" he asked, making a noise with his tongue as if he was checking he understood correctly. She ignored him and opened a few different pages from the search, highlighting where the figures differed.

By the time he finally got to see these number, he had already concluded that they were probably due to bad journalism rather than a fundamental flaw in reality. Instead, his interest was starting to grow in the many pictures she had around the room. Most of them were framed, but there were about a dozen that were just tacked onto the wall with pins. From how well dressed she appeared in the framed ones, Raxus was coming to the conclusion that these were more important to her than the others. But it was the unframed ones that were drawing his attention. On one of them it showed her pulling a ridiculous face alongside a similarly silly looking man. Both had their eyes wide open and mouths gaping, as if they were trying to mimic the skull of the creature that made up their background. She must have been at least ten years younger. The man was of a similar age and from their joyous, carefree demeanour around one another, they had probably been in a relationship.

All of this was irrelevant as his focus was on the skull in the background.

"What on earth is that thing?" he asked, leaning closer to the picture.

"My ex," she growled, only throwing a cursory look at where he was looking.

"The skull?" he asked, picking the photo off the wall. She scowled at the fact he was now picking things up, but did not stop him from looking at it.

"The dinosaur skull?" she asked. "A velociraptor or something. I think."

"Are there any of these things still around?" he asked, worried that these predators could be roaming outside. He had very scant knowledge of this time period and certainly less about the species that inhabited the era. He had clearly never seen the likes of a dinosaur.

"No," she shook her head. "They have been extinct for sixty million years..."

Her confidence in his sanity was starting to wane, now – at least as fast as her confidence in the strange woman in her kitchen. Plucking the photo back out of his hands, she put it on the desk and ventured back out of her office to check on Omega. She found the strange lady sitting next to her unpacked shopping bags, arranging the groceries into two neat piles.

"What are you doing?" Harmony whined, bending over to pick up a pack of carrots. Omega scowled at her and pointed to the other pile, holding a packet of coffee, a box of chocolates and a block of cheese.

"What are these?" she asked, as if she was having trouble identifying them. Harmony sighed and considered ignoring her question. She also considered calling the police again.

"Food of some kind," Raxus explained, stepping out after her. Harmony ignored them both and started picking up the items Omega had laid out across the floor.

"These three are peculiar," Omega declared, tapping each of their packets with a finger. "They are showing a form of demolecularization."

"How can you tell?" Raxus asked, leaning in over her to get a closer look. To his eye, they appeared normal.

"Demolecularization, indeed," Harmony sighed – as exasperated with the scifi babble as she was with their antics in her kitchen. "Please, can I put my shopping away?"

"Can I have this?" Omega asked, holding up the packet of coffee.

"No," Harmony replied, snatching it back out of her hands. She had already almost had one fight today over them.

"Hey!" Omega objected, snatching it back. "This is important!"

"Its my coffee. The only thing it is important to is my breakfast."

"Is there anything else that has this kind of demolecularization?" Raxus asked, squatting down to pick up the cheese. Harmony sighed and took a seat at the table, resting her elbows on it and her head in her hands. The thought about ringing the police still revolved around in her head, but at the moment she did not feel threatened enough by them to warrant it. She was more inclined to find out who should have been caring for them.

"Only in these three items," Omega explained, plucking the cheese out of his hands. "All off them are organic products."

"Interesting," Raxus replied, now picking up the chocolates. As Harmony looked up again, he began opening the cardboard box it was held in and looking inside.

"Hey!" she objected, grabbing it away from him. Omega immediately snatched it away from her and suddenly the three of them were on their feet in a stand-off around her chocolate. It was like the supermarket all over again.

"Will... you... stop stealing my *shopping!!*" Harmony screamed at them both. Very slowly, Omega started to put the chocolate back down on the kitchen table. An uneasy silence followed her actions, as Harmony tempered her anger and started thinking rationally about the two lunatics in her house.

"I am terribly sorry," Raxus apologized, "but this is very important. We may not have much time."

"Right, end of the world. Sorry," was the sarcastic response. Neither Omega nor Raxus were so far removed from the human condition that they did not recognize it.

"Would it help if we showed her the capsule?" Raxus asked, turning back to his colleague. "It might," Omega conceded. "They have enough of a concept of science here that they should be able to comprehend it."

Harmony shook her head and rested a palm over her temple, ignoring them both.

"We may be able to study the demolecularization better from there, as well," he continued. "I don't want to steal this lady's breakfast, though."

"Good grief," Omega shook her head – wondering why he was so bothered about offending the primate.

Raxus turned back to Harmony, who was trying her best to ignore both of them.

"Do you mind?" he asked, holding out a hand towards the opened box of chocolates.

"Mind? Mind what?" Harmony asked. Then, realizing he was going for the chocolate again, she shook her head. "Take it. Just go."

"The coffee and cheese as well?" Omega asked, already lifting the two packets.

"Please, allow us to explain," Raxus suggested, tentatively taking the chocolate. She watched him, but did not respond.

"Let's go," Omega shrugged, heading out of the kitchen. Raxus remained, leaning down to try and catch Harmony's gaze. She stared at the spot on the table where the chocolate had been.

"You seem like an intelligent woman," he began, as soon as he was sure she had seen him. "Perhaps if you came with us, we could explain to you what is going on. If we are right then you would not want to eat that stuff anyway."

"What do you mean?"

"It could well be poisonous."

She stared at him, realizing he was deadly serious.

"And you can prove that to me?" she asked, trying her best to sound as if she was entertaining the idea.

"Of course."

"I think I better warn you that I am a scientist. I am not going to be easily fooled."

She decided not to mention that her field was in particle physics, not biology or anything related to poisons.

"Even better!" he exclaimed. "You may even help us understand the problem!"

The sound of the front door closing cut their conversation short and Raxus emerged from the kitchen to find Omega had already left – with the coffee and cheese. Hurrying after her, he did not notice that Harmony had indeed followed.

He stepped out and dashed down her garden path, scurrying along with the chocolate box clasped in his hand. Harmony stopped at the threshold and watched as Omega rounded the end of the garden path, turned around the street corner and stepped directly into the strange monolith that had appeared there. She disappeared – either stepping behind it or somehow through it.

Harmony blinked a few times and peered around the edge of the door to get a better look.

There was no sign of Omega – she had stepped into the solid black slab and disappeared.

Then Raxus did the same.

Stepping out of the house, she cautiously looked over the road to see if any of the neighbours were spying. It must have been one of the few times that none of them were, as the street appeared deserted and as silent as it had when she had walked home.

There was no sign of Raxus nor Omega.

She made her way up the garden path, reaching the small wall that acted as the perimeter of her property. From here she could clearly make out the solid monolithic slab of stone and made sure that it was not concealing something behind it.

It was not.

Rounding the wall and making her way to the corner of the street, she stopped in front of it and looked up and down at it – wondering what it was and how it had got there. Most of all, she wondered how Raxus and Omega had hidden behind it and where they had gone.

Against her better judgment, she reached out a curious hand and tried to press her palm against it. She failed.

Instead of finding the cool resistance of the solid rock beneath her fingers, her hand passed directly through and emerged on the other side, as if there was a whole room hidden behind the black slab. Slightly off balance from the fact that her hand had not met resistance, she pulled back again and stared at the monolith in fascination.

Suddenly the scifi babble the two lunatics had been mumbling did not seem so ridiculous.

Wondering how much odder her day could get, she ventured forwards again and this time pushed her whole body through the inky black slab.

She was greeted on the far side by Omega and Raxus staring at her in surprise. Over their heads were three huge projections of numbers and graphs and a red and blue line hologram of her cheese, coffee and chocolate.

"How did you get in here?" Omega demanded. Raxus was reminded of his own reaction to Omega's arrival, not long before, in his laboratory.

"I just followed you..." she replied, hesitantly. "Its like its not really there..."

Her attention, however, was not on them nor her answer. She was completely transfixed by the holograms floating in the centre of the largely empty room.

"How did she get in?" Omega turned to Raxus, realizing she was in too much of a daze to answer.

"Closed time-like curve, allowing for her to have always been given access. We did inherit this capsule from a later version of ourselves, after all."

"What?" Omega asked, trying to get her head around time travel whilst at the same time trying to analyse what was wrong with the coffee.

"The capsule is caught in a loop," Raxus tried to explain. "It has already come back here with us and probably picked this young lady up at least once. When we drop it back again, an earlier version of ourselves will be waiting to pick it up and start the same journey all over again."

Omega stared at him with a look of horror mixed with confusion.

"Its a side effect of time travel. Closed time like curves exist everywhere – like a photon that loops back to hit two points at the same time. It happens naturally on the event horizon of a black hole – where the same photon can be detected in two places at once."

"This is not how the universe is meant to function," she complained. "You are telling me that there are other versions of us travelling up and down this timeline?"

"Ah, you see it is a bit more complicated than that."

"Excuse me?" Harmony cut in, finally finding her voice.

"Explain," Omega demanded, ignoring her.

"Each timeline has multiple universes attached to it, branching out from where different decisions are taken. If you affect the timeline, you create a paradox that branches out in another direction. Therefore, you can't return back to the point in time that you came from and affect the events before it. It prevents you from successfully killing your own grandfather, for example."

"Excuse me?" Harmony cut in again.

"So just by coming back here, we have created another simulation?" Omega asked, sill ignoring her.

"Simulation?" he frowned, shaking his head. "No. It creates an entirely new alternate universe, marginally different to the parent one."

"What is this place?" Harmony asked, this time stepping up to Raxus to interrupt them.

"I'm sorry," he smiled, politely at her. "Welcome to our capsule. We are trying to analyse the goods you gave us to see what the link is between them."

She frowned at him and looked down at the coffee, cheese and chocolate on the floor and then back up at the huge holographic projections of them. Shifting figures and graphs appeared all around the images, as if it was studying them from every angle from the atom upwards. It seemed an amazing amount of technology to her – especially when the link seemed so obvious.

"They are all Swiss," she explained, still staring up at the hologram.

"Swiss?" Raxus asked, as if the word meant nothing to him.

"Its a nation here," Omega explained - having the repository of all knowledge at her grasp, it was not hard for her to identify what she meant. Raxus, using his limited but still impressive intellect, could only guess what a nation was.

"I used to live there," Harmony explained – as if it was needed. "I developed quite a taste for the coffee."

"What is so significant about 'Swiss'?" Raxus asked. Omega was already realizing what it could be when Harmony confirmed it.

"Nothing, really," she replied, quite honestly. Her brain was now reeling through possibilities as to why these aliens would be interested in it. Of all the countries on the Earth, it had to be one of the least significant.

"A neutral territory in a mountainous area, surrounded by political allies," Omega frowned. "There is nothing in its known history to imply why it would be at the heart of the collapse."

"Its the home of the largest Hadron Collider in the world. I used to work there."

"That's it," Omega declared. "You have just started detecting Higgs particles there?"

"A few years ago, yes," Harmony replied, turning from the hologram to face her. "Where are you people from? You don't look like aliens."

"That is a long story for another time," Omega replied. "Raxus, set this thing a course for the Large Hadron Collider. I will feed you the local coordinates. Same time period."

Raxus waved a hand in the air and the holograms disappeared. A moment later and the entire room seemed to shake, drawing Harmony to rest a hand on the long sofa running around the edge.

Outside, it looked as if the monolith suddenly fell through a hole in the wall. One moment it was resting up alongside it, then suddenly it seemed to tip. As it passed through, it disappeared. A second later it was through the wall and dropping into the time vortex. A moment after that, it flopped into Switzerland, just outside of Geneva.

It materialized, wobbled and then rested. This time it was vertical, directly in the middle of a large field of sunflowers – sticking out among them exactly like a black stone slab would do.

Chapter Eight

The Mandela Effect

It was Jorge's turn to do the inspection. He wasn't happy about it, but then most people were unhappy about having to go to work at the best of times. When they asked you to potentially risk your health just to make sure some piece of technology was still working correctly, it really made you wonder what price they put on your life. In Jorge's case it was quite easy to calculate – the piece of machinery was worth about half a million dollars. Therefore, he figured, they thought he was worth somewhere less than this – as if he died, at least the machine would be okay.

It wasn't as if the machine was going to catch a virus.

He pulled his car off the road and into a pebble dashed courtyard, leaving the serene calm of the sunflower fields in his rear view mirror. He did not notice the black monolith sitting in the centre of the field and instead focused on the drab, industrial complex in front. A dozen huge silos of liquid hydrogen sat along one edge of the courtyard. A chain link fence with a colourful warning cut them off from the car park and he pulled his vehicle up next to this. Along the adjoining side was the entrance to the bunker-like facility that led to the heart of the complex. Next to that was a small, dilapidated looking hut that looked thoroughly out of place at the entrance of the largest, most expensive collection of scientific equipment in the world. He often wondered what it was doing there, at the entrance, but had never bothered to actually look inside it. Today would be no different.

He climbed out of the car and angrily slammed the door shut. Taking a moment to stand before the dull grey door at the entrance, he mumbled his curses about his boss and then started forwards. If all went well, he would not see another soul and would be out of there again in half an hour. He could then take the rest of the afternoon off, before his boss called him at five to check in.

He stopped at the door and started punching the combination into the electronic lock when he heard a set of footsteps approaching from behind. He turned, leaving the sequence half finished and stared in surprise at the three figures approaching.

"Harmony?" he asked, with a thick Austrian accent. She smiled sheepishly at him and waved from across the courtyard.

"Hey Jorge!" she nervously called back. "Its been a while!"

"Who are your two friends?" he asked, nodding nervously at them.

"They are here for a tour," she smiled at him. "Can you let us in?"

"We're in lockdown," he grumbled back at her, shuffling away slightly as they stopped within a couple feet of him. "We're supposed to keep our distance."

"What are you doing here?" she asked, keeping two meters away. Raxus and Omega seemed to completely ignore the social distancing rule and strolled right up to the door to start looking at the lock.

"I got the short straw. I have to check the photon accelerators." He fixed his attention on the other two as he spoke, who were now bent over the keypad on the door.

"Do you mind?!" he asked, suddenly breaking the social distancing rule to step in the way.

"I thought you were going to let us in?" the strange looking time traveller asked. Jorge turned back to Harmony.

"You know I can't let you in. You don't even work here any more."

"Really?" Harmony whined at him. "I mean, what damage could we do?"

"Millions of dollars worth," Jorge grumbled. But they both knew that was pretty hollow – there was no conceivable reason that she would do anything. She had a reputation and a career to her name, one that might still mean something once everything returned to normal.

"Who are the two goons?" he asked, nodding to the identically dressed pair at the door.

"Raxus and Omega," Harmony introduced them. Jorge frowned at both of them.

"Their names match their costume," he grumbled. "What are they? Scifi fans or something?"

"Well, they have converted me," Harmony replied, shrugging. She wasn't yet willing to voice the insane things she had just seen, nor question the fact that they had been transported to Geneva in the blink of an eye. Instead, she focused on smiling sweetly at Jorge and waiting for him to finally start unlocking the door again. He did so with a slight shrug and a shake of his head.

"Can't stand it, myself; Star Trek and rubbish like that. No realism."

"Right, no realism," Raxus nodded, pretending he had the faintest idea what he was talking about. He concentrated instead on what the Austrian was punching into the electronic lock.

"You aren't Trekkies, though, are ya?" he continued, not noticing the attention they were paying him. "I would recognize their stupid uniforms. What's yours? Space Wars or something? Jedi warriors?"

"Er, no..." Omega smiled politely when he looked up at her. "We are time travellers."

"Ah, Doctor Who. I should have guessed. What with the British accent and all."

"British accent?" Omega asked, suddenly aware that she had one. For the sake of convenience she had chosen a London accent when talking to Harmony. She switched suddenly to Austrian and asked if him if that was any better. He stopped unlocking the door in surprise at her fluent and perfect use of his mother tongue and started to ask where she was from. Harmony cleared her throat.

"Can we get in?" she asked, impatiently. Jorge mumbled something under his breath and finished the combination for the code. The door swung open.

It opened out into a huge industrial warehouse, with thin metal walkways all around the vast interior. Unidentifiable machinery cluttered the edges of the room, many covered in cheap plastic tarpaulin. Criss-crossing over their heads, the walkways converged with a group of coloured pipes around a huge lift shaft. This was currently closed off, with a large metal grate around its edges and a tiny platform and control at its centre.

Jorge grabbed a pair of safety helmets from their hangars on the wall and passed them to Omega and Raxus. They both stared at them, confused. He then took another pair and passed one to Harmony. She put it over her head and attached the chin guard, Jorge doing the same.

Looking between them, Omega and Raxus did also – both wondering what kind of protection the thin plastic hat was actually going to provide.

"It is not going to look like much down there," Jorge explained, leading them across to the lift shaft. "Its all been taken down for the upgrades. That was before the lockdown."

"It is planned to come back online next year," Harmony added. "I am still hoping that we can get a grant to come back again."

"Hoping these science fiction fans will fund you to make a warp drive?" Jorge joked. His humour did not amuse any of them.

"I am hoping to continue my research," she replied, ignoring his jibe. "Our government has promised grants but nothing has come yet."

"The lockdown stopped everything," Jorge sighed. "I feel your pain. We are probably looking at an extension for it to come back online. You probably have another year to get your act together before it matters."

He opened up the lift shaft and led them onto the platform. A few moments later it was rumbling into life and starting the long, slow drop into the heart of the complex. Omega and Raxus shared the same look again, wondering how many more quaint technologies they would be introduced to here.

"Have you spoken to Paul recently?" Harmony asked, referring to his boss. Jorge grumbled again.

"The bastard is the one who sent me down here. He's on his veranda at the moment, no doubt. Pretending to work by calling us all up and dragging us off the toilet."

"Painting a bit of a vivid picture there, Jorge."

"He is always on our back. He's only come down once and expects us to pick it all up for him."

"Who else is working at the moment?"

"Everyone's doing it remotely. As the whole facility was shut down for the upgrade there isn't really anyone who needs to come down at all. Makes me wonder if we can't just work from home until the upgrade is finished."

"So its just you here?" Raxus asked. Jorge looked over at him, wondering what the connotation of that comment was.

"No," he replied, hesitantly. "There's about twenty other people around the complex. Mainly technicians and support crew. Like me."

"You are neither," Harmony pointed out. "You're one of the best physicists here."

"Then why am I risking my life to check on a piece of machinery that nobody is using?" he asked, bitterly.

"Is that what you are doing?" Omega asked, surprised and a little horrified. "Is life that cheap here?"

"I am sure Jorge is exaggerating," Harmony held up her hand-worried they may be getting the wrong impression of their culture.

"Like hell I am," he complained, cutting her off. "Bastards don't care for us. They just care about the dollars they have invested down here."

"At least you still have a job," Harmony commented. "And Paul is not that bad a boss. You know that he would come down here if you asked."

"Bastard knows I won't ask," Jorge replied, sheepishly.

"And whose fault is that?"

"He is still a bastard."

"Much as I agree that all bosses are bastards," Omega cut in, "how long is this shaft?"

"It takes almost ten minutes to descend," Jorge explained. "I am sorry. You are probably expecting a tour?"

"It would certainly help," Omega nodded.

"Well ask her," he indicated at Harmony. "She knows it just as well as me. Probably a better talker, too."

"I don't know about that," she backed into the edge of the lift, coyly adding; "you talk pretty well after some red wine."

"Everyone talks rubbish when drinking."

"You have a knack for it. You went for twenty minutes about Nelson Mandela."

"And I will do so again. It is a conspiracy. He died in prison in the eighties. I remember it clearly."

"He was the President of South Africa," Harmony shook her head at him. "I still don't know how you missed that."

"I am not South African. But I can tell you how I know he died in their prison."

"Oh?"

"I remember seeing it on the news. It helped end the apartheid there."

"Nelson Mandela certainly did that," she nodded, still amused by his determination. "But he also became President afterwards."

"Its a conspiracy," Jorge shook his head. "Someone has invented that part for some reason."

"What possible reason could they have?!" Harmony laughed.

"Its an international conspiracy of Africans who want to take over the world using his false memory. They will probably bring him back to life with voodoo or something."

"Your nuts," Harmony shook her head. "And a little bit racist."

"You are the racist one," he countered; "forgetting the poor man's death, like that."

"Surely this could be settled pretty simply," Omega cut in, impatiently. "There is either an official record of his death in prison or there is not. You can't remember a news report if it never happened."

"That's part of the problem," Harmony sighed. "Somebody has clearly forged footage a news report of his death. I have seen it myself. It's easy to create. Any monkey with a laptop could have made it."

"Whereas the footage of his 'Presidential funeral' is so much more convincing?" Jorge countered, obstinately. "The guy doing the sign language isn't even making real signs!"

"That was..." she paused, trying to remember the actual footage herself. Frowning, she was finding it increasingly difficult to conjure any images of the scene in her mind at all.

"That was something else entirely," she shook her head. "It had nothing to do with the funeral."

"You do not seem so sure," Jorge snorted. "Maybe you think your memory is not so perfect?"

"Is this what you were talking about?" Raxus asked, after studiously observing the whole conversation. Harmony, still trying to concentrate on her ailing memory, looked over at Omega as well – suddenly worrying about how much the crazy woman had said was actually true.

"Did Nelson Mandela die in prison?" she asked, as if Omega knew. The other woman, from another time and another reality just stared blankly at her.

"I have no idea who you are both talking about," she admitted finally. For someone with an encyclopedic knowledge of almost everything that anyone could ever know, it was something of a humbling moment. It just made Jorge wonder what rock she had been hiding under to have never heard of Nelson Mandela.

"Who is he?" Omega asked, finally. Jorge snorted and answered for all of them.

"Probably one of the most important people in the fight for human equality in the last hundred years," he stated. "I thought Austria was bad. What the hell do they teach you people in England? Is it all Klingon and Business Studies?!"

He looked over her and Raxus's matching clothes again and turned away, watching the floors drop away.

"Is this what you meant by reality breaking down?" Harmony asked, whispering in the hope that Jorge would not hear. He did – and he started to turn back around to question the statement when Omega answered:

"Yes, I think it is."

"Reality here is already breaking?" Raxus asked, as shocked and terrified as he should sound at the concept. Jorge now stared at all three, wondering if they were playing some role-playing game or if there was a hidden camera filming his reaction.

"I am more concerned about why I know nothing about this 'Nelson Mandela' character?" Omega replied, looking to Raxus and then Harmony (when the former just stared blankly at her).

"I don't know what to say," she shrugged, when the others did not speak. "He was very important and very famous."

"I have a perfect recall of almost everything that ever happened to all known life in the universe," Omega stated (with more than a little pomposity). "Why do I not know about this man?"

All three of them responded at once – none of them grasping the importance of the statement and all three of them babbling something unhelpful in response.

"Wait, what?!" was Harmony's least useful reply.

"Should you?" Raxus asked - wondering why a single individual in the distant past would be important to an inter-dimensional traveller.

"You are a racist," was Jorge's contribution.

Omega stared back, slightly exasperated. For the briefest of moments she considered abandoning the simulation entirely and letting it play out to its inevitable destruction. She could then return back to her own reality, admit her defeat and wait for Alpha to deactivate her amalgamated consciousness.

"I have not been entirely honest with you," she turned to Raxus, opting to speak with the more evolved of the three.

"What do you mean?" he asked. "You have barely told me anything. You said you came from another reality and that the collapse is... well... for a lack of better words – *universal*. What is it you have not told me?"

She patiently waited for him to finish and then looked across at the other two, both of whom were now in a state of total confusion.

"I thought you were both time travellers," Harmony whispered. Looking at Omega, she whispered with a little awe: "What are you?"

Jorge just rolled his eyes, now determined that they were playing some kind of game based on Doctor Who.

"There is a lot I have not told you," Omega confessed to Raxus. "There is never going to be enough time to go through all of it. All you need to know right now is that I have a complete knowledge of almost everything that has ever happened or will happen. Yet I know nothing of this man."

The gravitas of her words were held with such a tone that he could not help but nod back at her, as if he grasped the importance. He did not.

"What do you mean?" he asked, still nodding. She rolled her eyes at him, much like Jorge was doing to all three of them.

"He is a fracture in reality. He is part of one time line but not of others, breaking the universe into two lines from one point. The fracture creates a weak point in the simulation, where data gets corrupted and duplicates with errors. Like in your equation."

"He is a paradox event?" Raxus asked, finally grasping what she meant. "He both died in prison *and* became President?"

"Which is why I know nothing about him. The event could not occur in my reality."

"Where there is no time travel."

"Wait, what?" Harmony asked again – interrupting as she was still taking in the entire conversation. "Now you can't even time travel?!"

"She comes from an alternative dimension where the laws of physics work slightly differently," he explained. He was quite familiar with the concept as his own laboratory had been capable of creating mini universes with alternative laws of physics. Harmony, however, was completely baffled.

"She is from an alternative universe?" she whispered. "Not just an alternate time line, but whole different reality?"

Omega thought about explaining further, but then decided against it. There was no point antagonizing them by explaining that their universe was simply a digital playground for her people to retire into.

"You are missing the point," she shook her head. "Your reality is already in a state of collapse."

"My reality?!"

"Our reality," Raxus interceded, as if to reassure her. "My era has already stopped existing. I am not entirely sure how I am continuing to exist."

"You are safe," Omega declared – as if she had the authority to do so. Placing a hand on his shoulder, she explained; "I copied you when I first arrived. You aren't going anywhere, no matter how much of your past gets deleted."

"You can do that?" he asked, staring at her. She looked down at the device on her wrist, which still hung there, dormant.

"I could."

"So what do we do now?" Harmony asked, still terrified by the idea of her reality collapsing.

"We are at the heart of the fracture here," Omega explained. "We test the interference patterns around the test site and we work out how large and how fast the fracture is growing."

"Interference pattern?" Harmony asked, wondering if she meant what she thought she did. Jorge also frowned and started listening more intently, as if he was suddenly concerned that their babble was not just a role-play game or some kind of science fiction homage.

"When light is projected through a series of dots, the single beam is broken up by the interference pattern – creating multiple dots from each hole. Its a basic observable test of quantum physics."

"We are quite familiar with quantum physics," Harmony nodded

"I should hope so," Omega growled. "The idea that you were tampering with a Higgs effect without knowledge of quantum theory would be insane."

"What are we supposed to deduce from the interference pattern?" Raxus asked.

"The fact that light waves are no longer stable," Jorge stated, with his back still to them. Omega raised her eyebrows, impressed with the answer.

"You have already observed this?" she asked, leaning around the big Austrian to look at his face. She could tell from the pained expression on his face that he was trying his best not to think about it.

"Yah," he sighed, finally and with a deep accent. "It was one of the last things we were testing before the closure."

"Have other laboratories replicated the experiment?" Harmony asked, looking worriedly between them.

"Not with any success," he shook his head. "It appeared to only be manifesting near to the site."

"Which makes sense," Omega nodded. "There are probably similar fractures all over the universe, wherever you people start tampering with the Higgs effect and the basic building blocks of your reality."

"You people?" Jorge asked, turning towards her suddenly. Wondering what he was offended by, she shrugged and added;

"People in your reality. It appears to be a flaw in the structure of existence that is easily manipulable."

"Whatever," he shook his head, ignoring her scifi babble. "We observed the effect in different stages at different depths on this shaft. The deeper we go, the stronger the effect."

"What is the effect?" Omega asked, now creeping around the lift to face him.

"It is a simple enough experiment," he shrugged again. "I could show you."

"Do so, please," she insisted.

Bringing the lift to a halt, he turned around and brought out a small box from his pocket. Lifting it to his right eye, he squinted through a small hole in one part of it and waited for his eye to adjust. Within the box was a tiny band of light, made up of a single large dot with a scattering of smaller ones falling from its sides into a faint rainbow of colour. For those who are not aware – this is a simple wave interference pattern, created when a laser is distorted across two closely positioned slits. It was one of the fundamental experiments to prove that light behaved as a wave.

He passed the box to Omega, who looked at the crude device and sighed. She had expected something a little more high technology, but admitted that the simple device did the trick.

The interference pattern looked normal to her – the same band of light and rescinding dots that Jorge had seen.

"Okay," she nodded, passing the box back. "I don't see anything unusual yet."

"If we had better equipment I could show you while we were moving," Jorge admitted. "Just wait while we drop a few hundred feet and look again."

He activated the lift again and the shaft seemed to judder as they began moving.

Harmony took the box from him and tried looking through as they descended, but the judder from the lift's descent prevented her from being able to make anything out properly. She passed Jorge the box back again, taking his arm to get his attention.

"Why didn't you release anything about this?" she asked, cautiously. He shrugged, partly out of a little guilt and then partly from resignation at the inexplicable.

"We tried to. We got it tested elsewhere and they just came up with a flat negative. When every other institution you ask tells you that your results are wrong, you have to assume that its the equipment."

"I think we are proving right now that it can't be the equipment that is faulty."

Jorge just shrugged again and looked helpless.

"Either we were wrong or physics works differently here than anywhere else in the universe." He shook his head, adding; "It is easier to believe that all your experiments are wrong."

Raxus nodded, he had particular experience of that kind of fear. Only a few hours before, he had been questioning his own experiments and how they were predicting the imminent end of the universe. If Omega had not appeared and assured him of his computations, he may have doubted them himself.

Jorge stopped the lift again and lifted the box up to his eye. Squinting for a moment, he left it there a little longer than needed and then sighed. Passing it over to Omega, he blinked a few times – as if what he had seen was still burned into his retina.

She took the box and looked into it, immediately spotting the difference from earlier. Where there had been a single band of steady dots, the was now a rippling blur. As she watched, the beams grew from the outside of the band and then morphed along towards the middle, as if they were travelling up and then back down the band.

This was not how light should behave. Both in the simulated version of the universe and in her own reality, light should behave in a normal, steady wave function. Where it hit resistance, as in between the slits in the box, it should ripple and create a steadily rescinding band of dots – as they had seen before. This strange movement of dots, rippling up and down the band, had significant ramifications for the stability of the reality they were standing in.

She put the device down again, blinking to test if it had affected her vision. Now that she was aware of it, she was almost sure that the light here seemed darker – as if it was not quite the same intensity as it had been a few hundred feet higher.

Harmony took the box from her hand and stared into it as well, determined to see what the fuss was about. She held it there a long time, staring into the strange band – marvelling both at its beauty and at the bizarre physics that must be at work.

Passing the box to Raxus, she also blinked a few times and drew her thoughts together.

"When was the last time you tested this and has the change manifested further out?" Omega asked Jorge, ignoring the other two as they both fathomed what the experiment meant. She was already more than aware of the consequences. It was indeed one of the signifiers that she had been looking for.

"We started noticing it directly around the collider; where the Tetraquarks were being created," he answered, grimly looking her and Raxus's 'uniforms' over again. He was becoming more sceptical about his earlier theory that they were simply science fiction nerds.

"Tetraquarks?" Omega asked, frowning. This was not a term that she was familiar with.

"Its the second significant discovery of the Large Hadron Collider. We think we may be close to proving the existence of higher dimensions."

"Its the first step towards creating the artificial realities from my time," Raxus cut in. His statement did more to reaffirm Jorge's original belief that they were science fiction fans than it did to help Omega understand what was being explained.

"We think there will be hexaquarks and decaquarks as well," Jorge continued, ignoring the comment. "When we start finding them, we can start including the extra-dimensional combinations that string theory have been harking on about for decades."

"This is all wrong," Omega shook her head. "The light bending, the multiverses and now your tertraquarks. Reality should not function like this."

"Its not our job as scientists to judge it like that," was Jorge's sober reply. "We just measure it and explain it as best we can."

The lift finally came to a halt and Jorge heaved the door open again. He stopped in mid step, blocking the route for the others. They all hesitated behind him, waiting for him to move.

"What is wrong?" Harmony asked after an awkward moment.

"There are people down here," Jorge stated, finally stepping out. He stopped again just outside the lift door, again blocking their way onto the corridor.

"There should not be anyone here," he continued. "The machines should not be running."

"Are they running tests?" Harmony asked, putting a hand on his back as if to reassure him. He just shook his head.

"Everyone should be in lockdown. That is why I am here. This is not right."

"That is what I am saying," Omega growled, as if the others should understand what she was already deducing.

"I am going to find out what they are doing," Jorge decided, decisively stepping forward into the corridor. "You should wait here."

"I am coming with you," Harmony insisted, worried for her friend. The other two followed anyway, Omega indicating to Raxus to step closer.

"What is it?" he whispered, trying to remain out of earshot of the other two.

"This reality is breaking down faster than I had anticipated," she explained, quietly. "The loss of those later eras must be creating shock waves. Either that or someone is smashing your different universes together."

"How long do you think we have?" he asked, worriedly looking around at the walls and ceiling as if he was expecting them to collapse and fracture as they had in his own time.

"I was rather hoping you could tell me," she shrugged. "I am still only a guest in this universe."

"I would need my equipment in the Capsule," Raxus explained. "And I would not want to bring it down here into an instability like the one causing the interference pattern. We could fall into a void or get lost in the Multiverse Wars."

"What are these tetraquarks?" she asked. "They seem to have something to do with crossing dimensions?"

"In my time we have not only proven the existence of multiple universes, we have also been invaded by them. They accused our universe of causing their collapse. Until you came along, we had always rejected the theory."

"You are quite definitely at the epicentre," Omega nodded. "That is why I came to you. Something is triggering the collapse in your time that is somehow related to the collapse here. I don't know what it is yet, but it has something to do with all of these extra universes cohabiting."

"And paradox," Raxus insisted. She glared at him, but had to admit that he was still (partially) correct.

"And paradox."

"Jorge!" a loud voice interrupted their quiet conversation. The other two stopped suddenly and both raised their hands, giving Omega and Raxus a brief moment to look around them and at the armed man facing them.

He was dressed entirely in black, with thick, heavy armouring over his chest, arms and legs and a matching helmet with tinted visor. Only his pale, thin lips were visible beneath it as even his chin was covered by a black strap.

"What the hell are you doing?" the armed man demanded, pointing his rifle at the confused looking scientist and his guests. "You know we should be in lockdown!"

"What?" Jorge asked, confused.

"You should be in mission control," was the stern response. "I am going to have to take your three friends into custody."

"Custody? What? Wait a minute!" Harmony objected, stepping up next to Jorge, despite the rifle being calmly waved in her direction. Raxus looked on worriedly, while Omega leaned against the wall with a sigh, ignoring the gun and the stand off to consider the greater consequences of all of existence collapsing around them.

"You can't be down here, ma'am," the armed man explained. "This is a restricted area."

"I used to work here!" she objected. "When did you start arresting people for coming down to take a look?!"

He ignored her and instead lifted his shoulder radio, clicking the device to open. Rattling off a series of numbers and codes into the device, he received a similar response a moment later.

"What was today's door code?" he demanded, levelling the gun towards Jorge. The Austrian scientist rattled off a series of numbers, keeping his hands high in the air.

"Okay. Come with me," he demanded, waving the rifle at them again. They raised their arms a little further and began shuffling past him and down the corridor. All except Omega, who still leaned against the wall, lost in her thoughts.

"Move!" he demanded, waving the gun at her. She distractedly looked up at him and then squinted down the corridor after Raxus and the other two. She followed them a moment later, her head stooped and her arms still folded as she pondered.

Her options for rescuing her child were rapidly diminishing.

Chapter Nine

Universe Hopping

The room they had designated as their control room was very different from how Jorge and Harmony remembered it. What had once been a server hall (one of the many dotted throughout the complex) was now converted into a huge office space. There were six desks around the room and a huge reinforced glass wall at one end, looking into the exposed core of the particle accelerator. A dozen computers sat on the desks, whirring at their operators - who were stooped over them. These were largely nondescript men and women of a variety of ages, none of whom were recognisable. There was an odd lack of chairs in there, especially considering the number of people stooped over desks and computers. But this was not the focus of their attention as they were led in. Instead, their focus fell on the one distinctly inhuman creature standing in the corner by the glass wall.

The Hybrid was immediately recognisable to Raxus and Omega. Jorge and Harmony just stood and stared in a mixture of horror and confusion.

It was bipedal like a human, but that was where the similarity ended. Its arms were coated in thick, black spikes that protruded from a similarly covered body. It had a strangely shaped head with an array of dull, dormant eyes. It stood rigidly to attention, as if it was nailed to the floor in the corner. The men and women in the office ignored it and continued their work – staring into screens and tapping at keyboards. Only one of them stopped to acknowledge their arrival.

"Another two?" he asked, straightening from behind his desk. He had thick rimmed glasses and looked as if he was a few years older than the others.

"We found Jorge with them," their guard explained. "The other woman claims she worked here."

"I doubt that," was his smirking response.

"What is going on here?" Harmony demanded, snapping out of her fixation on the Hybrid. Raxus and Omega exchanged nervous glances, both keeping their attention on the dangerous cyborg in the corner. It remained passive, staring into space – not breathing nor moving a muscle.

"You are about to see," was the calm answer from the man in the glasses. "If you care to wait a few moments we are conducting the next experiment."

"Experiment?" Jorge asked, joining in. "This place is meant to be closed down!"

"Closed down?" was the surprised response. Then a look of dawning understanding crossed his spectacled features.

"Ah. I see."

He turned to the guard, his expression changing to exasperation

"This is not our Jorge. That is why he was with the intruders."

The guard screwed up his face and then shifted it back between them.

"I asked him the door code. It is not as if he was with a floating ball of gas, this time. How was I supposed to know?" he countered.

"We must be getting closer to the root universe," was the resigned and sighed response. "It will be increasingly difficult to identify them."

"Who are you people?" Harmony interrupted again.

"And what is that thing doing here?" Raxus added, unable to contain himself as he threw an accusing finger at the Hybrid. It did not react.

"We are conducting an experiment," was the calm answer – ignoring the finger pointing and fear in Raxus's voice. "I don't know if you have noticed, but reality appears to be collapsing."

"At last," Omega sighed in relief – now joining in as well. "Someone else who spotted it?"

"And we are trying to do something about it," was the measured response. "We have had this conversation already."

"I am sorry?"

"You are Omega. He is Raxus. You escaped the far future because the multiverse is collapsing."

Both Raxus and Omega stared in surprise.

"This reality is no good to us," he continued, ignoring their surprise as if he had seen it all before. "Are we ready to initiate the next transfer?"

"Energy capacity is not yet at optimum," the Hybrid answered, making all four of them jump in surprise.

"What is that thing?" Harmony demanded, terrified of its spiky and inhuman visage.

"What is it doing here?" Raxus added, more aggressively. He knew how dangerous the Hybrids were.

"And who are you?" Omega added. "How do you know who we are?"

"Our reality is gone," he explained, tiredly. "We had to move to try and find one that could still stop or slow the collapse. The Hybrid is part of our universe and is helping us jump to the next."

"You are hopping universes?" Raxus asked. Jorge was now leaning back against the wall, wondering when he was going to wake up. The guard next to him apologised quietly; he was now also under arrest with the others.

"We use the Hybrid technology to amplify the atom smashers," the conversation continued around them. "This device is crude but it does the job."

"Smashing your way into another universe is likely to cause unspeakable damage," Raxus warned. "Its like opening the vortex with a sledgehammer."

"We have to use the technology available. The future has already stopped existing. Any damage we do pales in comparison to the collapse."

"How do you know who we are?" Omega asked again. He grimaced at her.

"My apologies, Omega. We have met a number of times already."

"You still haven't told me who you are?"

"I am the Director here. Professor Abrienne."

"And you survive the collapses by hopping to the next universe?" Raxus interrupted.

"It was your idea," was the startling response.

"My idea?!"

"Well, an alternative blob-like version of you from a future far beyond the capabilities of this universe."

"What?"

He did not get an answer as the Hybrid suddenly activated again, ending their conversation and causing the four of them to look over at it. When it spoke, it appeared to churn the words out mechanically – as if it was a machine.

"Optimal rift alignment reached. Power output is adequate. Activating."

"We are leaving your universe now," the man in the glasses explained. "I suggest you take a seat on the floor."

Looking around at the lack of chairs in the room, the four of them slowly lowered themselves down to the ground with the other occupants of the room. As the last of them sunk down to the ground, Harmony looked over to Omega – who shared her confusion.

"What is going on?" she asked, shifting her nervous gaze between her and the Hybrid.

Omega watched what they were doing, lowering herself on the floor as she stared at the variety of screens around the room. From what she could ascertain, they were using the combined power of multiple photon accelerators to smash particles together. Using the merged realities they had already gathered together, they were amplifying the forces massively – smashing the photons together at a magnitude eight times greater than what should have been possible.

"If I understand the situation correctly... they may be helping us," she answered. It had only taken a few heartbeats for her to calculate the forces involved and the potential result.

Harmony was about to ask another question when reality suddenly shifted.

The room seemed to vibrate slightly and then blurred, as if the ground was suddenly both in six places at once and simultaneously in none at all. The tiles on the floor merged with the ceiling panels and walls. The space between things was simultaneously infinite and nothing, making all things infinitely large and infinitely small at the same time. It was impossible to keep balance, even when sitting on the floor.

A moment later reality reaffirmed itself and there was quite definitely a floor again – just not where it had been.

Omega found herself slumped across the tiles, with her head resting on her right arm and her left sprawled around her back. With more than a little annoyance, she raised herself back up again and wondered how people dealt with having physical bodies at all. Despite her unfamiliarity with having a body, her and Raxus were the first to rise from the paralysis. This was largely because they were not physical creatures in the same way that everything else in the simulation was.

"Are you okay?" he asked her. She just threw him a look that said he should know better. Slowly the others started to rise up again.

"What just happened?" Harmony asked, holding her head.

Raxus stopped dead and stared at the Hybrid; whose eyes had suddenly lit up and was moving its spiked limbs. It stepped forward, rippled its many hair-like weapons across its body and spoke again:

"Transfer successful. New rift detected. Power supplies are nominal and charging."

The Hybrid shut down again once it had reported in, drawing Raxus to step cautiously towards it.

"Not so close," Abrienne warned him. "It is quite capable of defending itself."

"I was just going to take a look," Raxus objected.

"No you were not. I told you – I know who you are. You were going to try and kill It... if you could."

Raxus held his hands up defensively but could not state truthfully that he would not have tried if the opportunity arose. The Hybrids were the single greatest threat in all of time and space (next to the actual collapse of all time and space). He couldn't let it remain here without putting everyone's lives at risk.

"You do know what that thing is, right?" he asked, indicating to it.

"It has as much interest in maintaining reality as all of us," was the measured response. "We have had this conversation already."

"How?" Raxus asked, stepping forwards. The guard was there to take hold of his shoulder and stop him.

"Put those two with the others," Abrienne ordered, tiredly waving his question away. "We will try and decide what to do with the other woman and the other Jorge later. Leave them with the Hybrids for now."

"This way," the guard ordered them out of the door. Jorge was first through, obeying without question as he still tried to understand what was happening. Harmony was next, shaking her head and wondering if her day could get any stranger. Raxus threw a glance to make sure Omega was following and then stepped through after the other two, keeping his hands raised. Omega hovered for a moment longer than necessary but followed the others out when the guard waved his gun at her. She did not care for the threat, but chose to go on her own terms: She was curious about the fact that there were 'others'.

Raxus stared around the room in mute fascination. He had not expected to be sharing a room with such an unusual array of himself.

To his left was an exact clone of himself – appearing almost exactly like him – as if they had chosen the same body-fit when they had got up. Though this was unlikely, it was not unheard of – a little like two people turning up in the same suit and shirt to work on the same day. Unfortunately there were three others that were all almost exactly the same as him.

Then there was the large ball of talking puss in the centre of the room, currently dominating the conversation in a surreal discussion. Its method of propelling parts of its body into the air in tendrils made its display almost hypnotic. The booming voice it used to project its view dominated their attention. The fact that the blob had a voice at all – his voice – just added to the surreality.

To the left of the huge blob was a reflective gas that occasionally added to the conversation by coughing out words. As it did so, it threw accusatory flickers of light around the room at him – as if it was trying to reflect the light around its body into a spotlight. He did not know what it was, but he definitely got the feeling that it did not like him.

The one that caught his attention the most was the eight limbed creature with his face. It was as if he had been transplanted onto a huge body of legs, whilst the rest of his body remained relatively in proportion. It was currently a silent member of the discussion, resting back on four of its legs, whilst rubbing two of its fore ones together like it was scheming.

It was at this point he decided to remove the safety helmet, noting that the other versions of himself had done the same.

Omega, Harmony and Jorge had all been taken to other rooms. He did not know if they were currently facing a similar assault on the senses, but he doubted it.

They had all turned and glared at him when he entered, complaining (like Abrienne had) of 'another two'. What this meant was lost on him as they immediately went back to discussing how the 'experiment was doomed to fail'. It took him the next couple minutes (along with staring at the strange clones and warped manifestations of his features around the room) to work out they were talking about universe hopping.

"There are only so many times they will be able to do this before they start breaking their little bubble," the conversation continued.

"Not much we can do about that," was the nonchalant response from the blob. "If they break it we will go with the rest."

"I don't understand how we still exist, anyway?"

"We are safe now that we are out of our universe," the gas explained, as if it knew what it was talking about. "The collapse may be happening here, but it is a different collapse."

"What happens when we get swallowed by a foreign universe's collapse?"

There was a moment of silence as they considered this and Raxus took that lull to enter the conversation.

"How many times have they done this?" he asked, looking around them. There was a shared sigh and the conversation continued, ignoring him.

"We think its eight times so far," the one to his left replied, quietly. "There are eight of us here. It stands to reason."

Raxus nodded, realising that there were indeed eight different individuals in the room. And all of them were different versions of him. This fact was not so hard for him to get his head around – being that his era was under threat of invasion from other universes already. Those universes had all been close enough to spawn very similar versions of reality – making him expect more clones.

"Why are we gasses and blobs?" he asked, indicating the stranger of the eight manifestations. He ignored the silent spider in the corner.

"Reality is versatile."

Raxus nodded to himself and then looked over at his doppelgänger and nodded again, slowly coming to realise what was happening. Every time they hopped through another universe they found another version of him and Omega there, doing the same thing. There could potentially be an infinite number of them, which would make their task significantly easier. Two heads maybe better than one, but infinite heads are infinitely better.

"What is the Hybrid doing there?" he asked. His double (we shall call this one Raxus[1] for the sake of distinction. This form of distinction will become more important later, so necessary emphasis is being placed here; on this particular version of Raxus) scowled when he brought it up.

"We don't trust them either," he replied. "But we have to admit, it has every reason to want to continue existing as well. We assume that there is a ceasefire until this catastrophe is averted."

"It's up to something," Raxus affirmed. "It will stab them in the back."

"We know. The gas version of us tried to kill it and then tried to kill the Director. It didn't work."

"It has not helped him trust us, either."

"I don't think he was going to trust us anyway. Omega has rubbed him up the wrong way half a dozen times already."

"There are other Omegas?"

"One for each of us. She brought us all here, basically. Or we brought her here. She kept us from being blinked out of reality when our era collapsed."

"Do any of you know how she did that?"

"No. That matter is also part of the debate..."

He stared around the room again and hoped that Omega was having more luck.

Chapter Ten

A Fistful of Omega

There were eight of her, each mirroring the appearance of Raxus's doubles from eight different realities. The gaseous and blob ones were by far the most annoying of all of them. They had already established their own hierarchy, based on how long they had been there and what they had consequently deduced. They dominated the discussion, barely giving her any attention when she arrived and dominating the other more human looking versions of herself with their blustering confidence.

She was getting on quite well with the spider version, however. Its strange appearance meant nothing to her – indeed her own physical body was still something of a novelty. Shuffling in next to its huge head and long limbs, they shared their own quiet discussion whilst the others had theirs.

The first thing that they had established was that none of them were real. This was actually obvious when considered – all of them shared the memory of entering the simulation and therefore none of them believed that this was real. It had taken them a little longer to agree that none of them were the original version of Omega. This was where the conversation became a little harder to follow. It is also the point when our Omega entered and very quickly created her own side discussion with the Spider to work out what was going on.

"But how can you have come from the year twenty billion?" she was asking. "The simulation ended four billion years before that."

"That was the first hint there was something wrong," the spider replied, with unnervingly good English. "Three of us worked out that we were simulations pretty quickly."

"Simulations?"

"I am definitely a simulated version," the Spider affirmed, confidently. "We have already worked out that none here could be the original."

"How can you be so sure?"

"The Hybrids are pushing up through the boundaries of reality towards the original simulation. As they get closer we see closer and closer approximations of the root version. That's why your simulation ended at sixteen billion and ours did not. Ours was a simulated version of the simulation."

"So the reality you were in was further from the original?"

"We are trying to number them, but with little idea of how many there are it seems pointless. Ultimately, Universe Zero is the one that created the simulation. That is the one the real Omega came from. Universe One is the simulated universe that we actually entered. Universes two to infinity are the ones the simulation created. We are all from one of the universes in this range."

"So none of us are real?"

"Well, we are as real as anything in the simulation. But yes, we are just simulations of Omega – not the real thing."

"Makes a girl feel like having an existential crisis..."

"Yeah. We have all done that. It got a bit ugly when the blob and the gas-thing were arguing it out. That's why I stay quiet, now. They really hated it when more human-like versions turned up like you. It proved they definitely did not exist."

"So why are you a spider?"

"The further down the simulations from Universe Zero, the more different the reality. Our simulations lasted longer – allowing for more variants to survive and push out from the collapse."

"So you, the gas and the blob versions were here first?"

"Yeah. Then the others like you started showing up – proving the fact that we were pushing upwards through the chain. One came from a reality where the Earth was flat – they also worked out they were in a simulation."

"Flat Earth?" our Omega asked, sceptically.

"It appears that the simulations allow for a number of more ridiculous types of existence."

"Why were all the people in the control room like me? Shouldn't they be blob-like if they were first?" she asked, ignoring the ridiculousness of the situation. She was talking to a giant spider version of herself, after all.

"The group in the control room are all from this era; around thirteen billion," the spider explained. "We all come from an era beyond sixteen billion, where the dominant forms of life are ultimately different. The more different the reality, the more different the later diversions. The only consistent thing through all of them seems to be these Hybrids."

"And they are pushing us up through another reality at the moment?" our Omega continued.

"As far as we can tell. The first realities were a far cry from what Universe Zero actually looks like. Once we broke through from the Flat Earth reality, we started getting into the core versions. Like yours."

"And these realities spawn more because of their ability to time travel?"

"Yes. These are realities spawned by an infinite number of possible simulations. Each of them then have their own infinite numbers of alternatives according to the choices of the near infinite number of beings that inhabit the simulation."

"So there are an infinite number of infinite possibilities?"

"As the collapse continues it will steadily reduce those to one. Or none."

"Which leaves us with our problem," our Omega stated. "It should not be collapsing at all."

"We still can't find the core reason."

"And none of your bracelets work?"

The spider shook its strangely shaped head and shuffled its legs around to show the dormant device. It looked very similar to the one around our Omega's wrist.

"None of them. All of them broke at the same time. We figure the simulation removed the access as we would destabilise the simulation of the simulation. If that makes sense?"

"Barely. So the real version of us will still be able to use their bracelet?"

"Theoretically speaking. Unfortunately we are just simulations of ourselves, so we are bound by the rules within the simulation. If the simulation wants us to be able to use the bracelet then we can. I imagine the program in Universe One has restricted the original Omega in the same way."

"You are speaking as if you believe the simulation has a will of its own?"

The spider seemed to smile – a disturbing visage to see on a warped version of her own face.

"We think it does," was the disturbing response. "From what Raxus told us, they created their own simulated universe using an AI to run it – very similar to our own child. Just as they got it running, everything started to collapse."

"My Raxus mentioned this," she nodded. "We were trying to get to it when their bubble universe collapsed."

"Same with all of us. We are probably simulating what the real Omega would do."

"So we just wait until the Hybrids reach the original simulation?" our Omega asked, dubiously. There were many things with that plan she did not like – not least the standing around and waiting part.

"They seem to be doing our job for us," the Spider stated. "The blob version of us seems to be convinced they will succeed."

"What do you know about these Hybrids?"

"Only what my Raxus has told me," she shrugged all eight of her shoulders in a ripple. "They are aggressors in their universe but appear to be of a unified integrated intelligence – much like ourselves."

"My Raxus sees them as an enemy. Can we trust them?"

"It can only be in their best interest to maintain reality," the spider affirmed. "Why would they want to encourage their own destruction?"

"I still have misgivings," our Omega growled.

"Of course. So do we all. We share the same mind."

"There is something about their integrated consciousness passing through multiple realities that concerns me. Who knows what kind of intelligence could be borne from it."

"It is very similar to us all gathering here. We have at our disposal eight times the collective intelligence of our universe."

"I suppose we can take heart in the fact that so far we have established very little..."

"Are you two quite finished?" the blob version of Omega demanded. It was difficult to see its face, buts its eyes bore down on her in a huge reflection of her own. The rest of the room had turned to stare at them as well, as if they were the naughty pair at the back of the classroom.

"I think I have caught up, yes," our Omega responded, confidently. "Have you managed to decide what we are going to do next?"

The silence that descended spoke volumes.

"Come on!" our Omega cried out, exasperated. "Each of us has the combined intellect of more civilizations than have existed here. Between us we should be able to come up with something?"

"We are not familiar with the rules of these simulated simulations," the blob grumbled – as if making an excuse for them all.

"Our Raxus was our link to how each simulation worked," another one (Omega^6) continued. "That was why we copied him."

"And that is why we have been separated?" our Omega asked, poignantly.

"Another reason we should mistrust the motivations of the Hybrids," the spider added. "Why would they want to separate us if we could help them?"

"We did not exactly endear ourselves to the Director," the gas vibrated.

"I do not think the Director has much influence," our Omega shook her head. "The Hybrid – for all that it seemed to be dormant - seems to call the shots here. They are by far the superior race."

"And there were many more of them throughout the complex," the spider added, stepping up behind the smaller, human version. "They all look dormant, but they probably outnumber the organics."

"I think we need to talk to our Raxus," Omega added.

"If we start disobeying, we are going to antagonize the situation," the blob chastised them. "At the moment their actions are helping us."

"We think they are," the spider countered. "We can't be sure of anything while we are stuck in this room."

"We are hardly stuck," the gas pointed out. "We can all leave at any time."

"But we risk antagonizing them," the blob countered again. "I for one do not think this would be a wise action at present."

"And how long do we wait?" the spider angrily chittered its limbs. "Until reality collapses and the simulation fails?"

"If that is what must happen," the blob responded. "At that point our simulations will end and the real one will be the only one left."

"Assuming that the real one does not get trapped in this same situation?"

At that point another Omega entered the room. Looking around herself with surprise, she then shared the same dawning realization that they had all felt when they had first entered. The discussion began again.

Harmony had a very different experience from the others.

She laid sight on no doppelgängers of herself, nor warped versions from other realities that resembled spiders, blobs or gasses.

Omega and Raxus had been directed into different rooms and left there, the latter giving them one last worried look before they had closed the door on him. Jorge had held her hand, led by the guard through the corridor. They were marched further into the complex and passed a number of the sinister looking Hybrids. All of them seemed to be dormant, just like the one in the control room – standing at the edge of corridors and entrances of rooms. Their limbs were drooped and the arrays of spikes over their bodies were all pointed downwards. It was as if they were waiting for something.

Jorge's hand tightened on hers. The guard nudged them around the corner and into another corridor, away from the sinister creatures.

They were led into a large chamber, that had once been a server room. The computers had been removed and scuff marks on the floor showed where they had laid. There were a set of three steps leading down into a large, oval area in its centre. It looked like something had once sat there, but had since been removed. Their attention was drawn away from this and towards the periphery. There were twelve recesses in the circular wall, each occupied by another of the strange and hideous Hybrids. They were all dormant, each of them resting with their backs against the wall and limbs by their side. They did not move and their eyes (for most had several) appeared to be closed.

The guard shut the door behind them.

"Now what?" Harmony asked, staring around herself.

"Am I dreaming?" Jorge asked. "I honestly don't know any more."

She took a step back towards the door, pressing her hand up against it to see if it would push open. It did not move and the handle appeared to be jammed when she tested it. She guessed that they were locked in there, meaning that they intended for them to stay with the (presently) dormant creatures.

Seeing that she was not answering, Jorge started to make his way around the edges – avoiding getting too close to the recesses and their eerie occupants. The dim lighting made their visages all the more sinister in the shadows.

Harmony gave up on the door and slumped onto one of the steps. Putting her chin in her hands, she rested her elbows on her knees to prop her head up and sighed. This was not how she had expected her day to go. Jorge was in a similar state, muttering to himself, pacing the room and trying not to look into the recesses. Every now and then he would get out his mobile phone, check the signal (as if he expected to get one down here) and then put it away again. He managed a few laps of the room before he also slumped onto the steps, next to her.

"What are we supposed to do?" he asked. "Are we prisoners? Who are these people? What are they doing here?"

She had no answer that would make sense so she remained silent, staring blankly across the oval floor. She was about to try the door again, when the lights in the room brightened suddenly.

The Hybrids all came to life at once, moving as one as if they were controlled by a single entity. Their right legs moved forwards and all of them stepped out, their arms moving mechanically to maintain their balance. It was like watching twelve clockwork soldiers marching in unison.

Harmony and Jorge scrabbled towards the door, pressing against it in the hope that it might fall open.

The creatures stopped after taking two steps out, all of them now on the perimeter of the steps to the central oval area. Their many bright eyes stared directly ahead, glowing with an artificial aura.

"Analysis complete. Re-convergence confirmed. Parameters for second stage have been met. Course set for Universe One."

They spoke in unison, like twelve choir singers artificially unified with a voice harmonizer. It was slightly beautiful, but made sinister when they all stepped back into their recesses again. They immediately seemed to shut back down.

"What was that?" Jorge asked. Harmony shared a scared look over her shoulder at him.

"I don't know," she admitted, "but I have a feeling we are about to find out..."

There was a moment of silence as the two of them stared around themselves, expecting an explosion of activity – or just something to mark the fact that something had changed. Nothing did. Silence pervaded the room, the Hybrids remained in their recesses and Jorge just stood next to her – a strange expression of confusion, fear and desperation on his face. She was just about to give up on expecting anything to happen when something did in fact happen.

It started with a thump from somewhere outside – the dull thud of something large hitting a wall. It was rapidly followed by a strange screaming; the type that was made when a blade was dragged against a solid iron surface. They both winced and slowly stepped away from the door, keeping their backs to it. They kept their gaze on the strange Hybrids in their recesses, not daring to look round at where the noises had come from.

The door burst open and the guard propelled himself through it and into their backs. The force of his careless careening carried them with him in a flailing mass of bodies. Throwing both of them forwards, he fired his rifle at something in the doorway. They did not see what he was shooting at, as by the time they caught their balance, he had slammed the door shut again. He dropped to one knee, gun trained and head bent down to aim.

There was a moment of calm as his heavy breath permeated the air and the other two regained their balance.

"What the hell?!" Harmony exclaimed, swinging around as she staggered into the centre of the room. Her exclamation was enough for the guard to throw her a glance, whilst keeping his gun and his attention trained on the doorway. His gaze flitted past her, however, and widened into horror as he remembered what else was in the room with them.

He was swinging around to face the Hybrids when the door burst open. He stopped in mid swing, attempted to turn back and was abruptly filled with spikes as a barrage swept from the doorway and into his body. Several slid straight through him – spattering the ground with blood and tiny, sharp spikes. The guard continued his spin and spiralled down into the floor, carried by both his own momentum and the many spikes that had just been shoved into his flesh. By the time he finished sliding over the bloody surface, he had stopped twitching entirely.

The twelve Hybrids in the room remained dormant, their limbs at their sides.

Harmony screamed, backed away and then stopped when she realised her actions were taking her closer to the dormant monstrosities in the recesses. She threw her hand over her mouth to stop herself yelling further (and for fear of awakening the creatures). Jorge just stared in horror and looked up at the doorway. He was just in time to see the Hybrid turn away and move down the corridor, out of sight. Its spikes seemed to regenerate as it did so.

"What is going on?" he asked, looking first at Harmony and then around the room at the dormant creatures. They did not seem bothered by his gaze, nor the abrupt execution of the guard in front of them.

"We need to find the other two..." Harmony panted, lowering her hand from her mouth. She could not take her eyes from the body and the rapidly expanding pool of blood.

"They were as crazy as this lot," Jorge growled. "And made about as much sense."

"That is why we need them," she insisted. "They might be crazy enough to understand it."

"Are we dreaming?" he asked, staring into the recesses around the room.

"Maybe," was her less than encouraging response. "Come on. The door is open, now."

She clenched her fist and stepped past the body, finally dragging her eyes away from it. With steadily growing determination, she made her way up to the open doorway and peeked outside.

The corridor beyond was empty in both directions. There were some grazes in the wall near the door and a few of the Hybrid's spikes sticking through it, but no movement nor sign of the creature that had fired them. She stepped out, signalling for Jorge to follow. He did so, backing out and keeping his attention on the twelve dormant recesses. None of the Hybrids in the room moved nor reacted to them – as if they had finished with them or no longer cared about their presence.

"Which way?" she asked, staring one way and then the other. There was the echo of gunfire, but she could not be sure which direction it was coming from.

"We came that way," Jorge affirmed. "Through the server sections."

He led her towards an increasingly loud rattle of gunfire, pausing at the corner of the corridor to check around it. There was no sign of the Hybrids that had stood along the walls. The rattle of gunshots were diminishing – not with volume, but with intensity.

"All clear," he whispered back to her, picking his way around the corner. There were signs of conflict everywhere. Spikes stuck from the wall and discarded shells lay around countless bullet holes. Leading her along that section, he came to the next corner and hesitated again. The gunshots were now diminished to an occasional flurry, interrupting the silence like a drill. He waited for the latest burst to die down, letting his heart and breath settle before summoning the courage to continue. He was about to swing around the corner when Harmony grabbed his arm.

"Someone is coming!" she hissed at him, backing away and pulling him from the corner. He heard the footsteps a moment later and staggered back a few steps with her. She ducked into a nearby doorway, pushing on it to see if it was locked. To her relief the door fell open and she hurried inside.

Jorge continued backing up the corridor and almost missed the fact that Harmony had ducked into the doorway. He was about to follow when Director Abrienne came around the corner of the corridor with someone. Someone who looked very familiar.

He stopped and stared at himself, as the new duo slowed and spotted him.

"What the hell?" he asked in unison with himself.

"What are you doing out here?" Abrienne demanded. Jorge could not take his eyes off himself and ignored the question to reiterate his own. The duplicate version of him did the same thing.

Just when he thought things could not get any stranger, the air sparked in front of him and something started to materialize there. At first it seemed to just be a group of spinning discs, gears and wheels, hovering in the air as metallic clumps sparked into existence around them. Within moments it was solidifying, sealing over the cavities whilst revealing several spinning cogs. As its arms and legs appeared, its head took form as well – revealing cold, mechanical eyes and a crude mouth-like slit. It turned its attention to the two Jorges.

"What the hell is that?!" the Director exclaimed. Nobody answered and it raised one arm and pointed at the new Jorge, standing next to him. A moment later he no longer existed – as if there had never been a doppelgänger standing there. There was no puff of smoke, no beam of energy nor blast of power. He simply ceased to exist.

"Er..." Jorge began, holding up his hands as the clockwork machine turned to face him. His mind was falling over itself as he desperately tried to keep track of what was going on and who was trying to kill who. He was pretty sure he had no idea who the new faction of clockwork robots were. He was also quite sure he had no idea who these Hybrids were supposed to be. He decided the best course of action would be to ask this newcomer if he could help in any way and hope that it was not a psychotic robotic killer with the sole purpose of wiping him from existence.

"...Er... can I-"

He never got to finish the question as the strange clockwork robot wiped him from existence.

The Director raised his hands, at a complete loss of what to do next. Harmony watched from the doorway of the server room – in an equal or greater state of confusion.

"Look," the Director began, keeping his hands up, "I do not know what you want and I do not know what the Hybrids are up to, but-"

He was also cut off in mid sentence as the mechanical man promptly removed him from existence. Harmony gasped and ducked back into the room, slamming the door shut as she did so. Desperately trying to get a grip on the situation, she sunk down to the floor.

Omega's patience started running out some time before the conversation completed its inevitable loop back to the discussion she had just had. Leaving the others to continue their pointless debate, she marched up to the door and tested its strength. Finding it locked was not an issue. She put her shoulder up against it, applied just the right amount of force and a moment later was forcing it open and almost taking it off its hinges.

"What do you think you are doing?!" the blob version of herself demanded.

"I am leaving," she explained. A burst of gunfire echoed into the open room with her, as if to punctuate her sentence.

"What was that?" the spider version asked.

"Gunfire," was the obvious and inevitable response from another version.

Then a Chronobot shimmered into existence in the centre of the room. At first it was just a few sparking cogs and wheels, shifting into existence in mid-air. Then the rest of its metallic body started appearing around it, showing the frame and then the arms and legs.

"Any of us know what those things are?" the blob Omega asked, as it completed its materialization.

"Raxus said they were Chronobots," the spider replied. "Apparently they guard the time vortex from paradox, but they seem a little whimsical in their policing."

There was a general murmur of consensus between the other Omegas when the Chronobot raised its arm and pointed at the spider version. None of them paid this action much heed to begin with and they were about to continue their discussion regardless (much to our Omega's exasperation) when the spider stopped existing.

The reaction that went through the various Omegas was one of complete panic. The blob reared back in a wave whilst the gas dispersed itself towards the door at a great speed. The human-like versions of Omega all scrabbled away from the area the spider had just occupied. The Chronobot then pointed at one of them and they likewise disappeared – as if they had never stood there.

Our Omega now bolted from the doorway, rapidly followed by the expanding wave of gas. The blob was the next to disappear –

incapable of slurping its way through the doorway before the Chronobot pointed at it.

"How the hell did it just do that?!" the gas was shrieking in various colours. Our Omega ignored it and started wishing she had bolted the other way up the corridor. They seemed to be going deeper into the complex and away from the entrance. There was a corner coming up, which she hoped would lead back round towards the control room. Checking over her shoulder, she spotted the most recent version of herself stagger out of the doorway. They took no more than a step through the threshold before they also disappeared.

"Its like they stopped existing!" the gas continued to shriek in more violent colours. Omega could see something stepping up to the door. The corner of the corridor was still a few steps away.

"Nothing in this universe should be able to affect-"

The gas version was cut off as it also promptly disappeared. The Chronobot, now standing in the doorway, shifted its attention towards our Omega. She fell around the bend in the corridor before it could point and charged deeper into the complex.

She needed to find Raxus.

Her fears for her child has suddenly been amplified. Before now she had just been worried that the illness in the program might be incurable. Now she was worried that the program was trying to delete her as well. What was worse – she was pretty sure she was just another aspect of her own program, imagining what she would do within the simulation. She was no more real than anything else in the simulation. This explained why the simulated Chronobots were capable of deleting her other manifestations. It also explained why the device on her wrist stopped working and why nothing in this reality made much sense.

She barely noticed the dead guard as she careened around the next corner and paid even less attention to the Hybrid standing over the body. It did not ignore her, however. Its entire body seemed to shimmer in reaction to her presence, the many spikes across its body all swinging towards her like magnetized iron filings. Its bright, artificial eyes blazed – some kind of programmed malice lingering in its depths.

Hundreds of tiny spikes flew out from the Hybrid and spattered across her body, puncturing it like thick, black hairs.

Omega slowed and stopped, staring in surprise at the array of spikes sticking through her. That surprise quickly shifted through relief (as she realised that they could do her no harm) to anger (that the Hybrid had slowed her down). On the other hand, it looked quite surprised that its attack had done nothing. It then looked terrified as she bore down on it, picking up speed as she continued up the corridor. It backed away, rapidly replenishing its spikes in order to fire again.

She grabbed it as she passed, picking it up with both hands and ignoring the spikes growing through her fingers. Digging her nails in to get a good grip on the creature, she then tore it into two pieces, ignoring the spray of oil and bodily fluids that pumped out. Holding the two halves of its body in the air for a moment, she waited for it to stop twitching. Without slowing her pace, she tossed the remains down the corridor and continued on her way.

Her patience had finally run out.

Chapter Eleven

What is Universe One?

Raxus threw the door open and promptly fell over Harmony, who was slumped down next to it. She yelped, he yelled and the two of them went rolling over the floor.

"What the hell?!" she shouted, as angrily as she was surprised.

"What are you doing?" he exclaimed back at her, trying to pick himself up off the floor.

"Hiding!" was her obvious response. "What is going on out there?!"

"I wish I knew," he replied, shaking his head at her. "It is complete chaos. There are Chronobots, doppelgängers and Hybrids and everyone seems to be killing everyone else."

"I only know what doppelgängers are. The rest of this is Greek to me."

"What is Greek?" he panted.

"Where is Omega?"

"I don't know," he shook his head. "I took off as soon as the slaughter began. Where is Jorge?"

She shook her head, mutely confirming that he was no longer with them. Not willing to press on the matter, Raxus crept back up to the doorway and peeked through – making sure the way was clear. The corridor was silent, though the sound of gunfire clattered from further within the complex. Harmony winced at it and shuffled a little further inside, ducking behind one of the whirring computer cabinets. He remained at the door, unwilling to open it any further but determined to see as much as he could. Shuffling his feet, he tried his best to see as far as possible. He could not be sure, but he thought he saw movement coming from the far end.

"What is it? Do you see something?" she asked, sensing his change in demeanour.

"Be quiet!" he insisted, still trying to get a better vantage. She did as she was told and crawled towards the door to try and see through. He did not notice that she was now poised behind him, looking between his legs and through the gap.

Omega hared into view, immediately spotted Raxus spying through the door and made a bee-line straight for him. He straightened in surprise, tried to back away from the door and tripped over Harmony again. The two of them rolled over the floor in a heap, with him on top. Omega then burst in and immediately tripped over both of them.

"What are you doing?!" she exclaimed as she picked her way back out of their pile on the floor.

"We were trying to hide," Raxus growled back at her. "I don't know if you noticed, but all kinds of chaos has broken out."

"Oh, I noticed," Omega replied confidently. "I just saw several duplicates of myself disintegrated."

"I had a very similar experience," Raxus confirmed, now getting back on his feet. Harmony slumped against the closest computer cabinet, opting to remain on the floor.

"Those Chronobots seem to be targeting us," Omega continued, closing the door after checking the corridor was still clear. "What exactly are they?"

"I don't really know," he confessed. "Nobody does."

"What do you mean?" she asked. "This is your reality. You said yourself that they serve some kind of purpose? Preventing paradox?"

"But there has never been any logic in their actions," Raxus insisted. "They don't seem to care about some paradox events."

"But they are hostile to people who create paradox?"

"Most of the time. Hybrids seem to get away with it more than anyone else, though."

"I figure eight different versions of us in one place might constitute a paradox," Omega stated, drily. "The Hybrids smashing through realities might well attract their attention as well. If not from their universe - then at least from one of the universes they are smashing their way through."

"But the Hybrids and Chronobots ignore each other," Raxus stated. "They don't seem to care about each other at all – just everyone else down here."

"So they are working together?" Omega asked. "Then why were the Hybrids pretending to work with the dumb humans at all? And why did we see them destroying each other back at your tribunal?"

"I have no idea. Maybe the parameters of the mission here changed?"

Harmony, who had been watching the conversation mutely from the floor until this point, now suddenly decided to join in – pretending that she had some idea of what was going on. By some complete chance of fate (or so it would appear at this point), she happened to say something of immense importance to the conversation.

"They said 'Parameters for second stage have been met. Course set for Universe One.' I think."

Both Raxus and Omega slowly turned their attention to her, glaring down on her big, bright and wide eyes as they stared innocently back up at them.

"I think..." she reiterated.

"Universe One?" Raxus asked.

"Who said that?" Omega demanded.

"Those Hybrid things. Right before everything started going weird," she winced, adding the emphasis; "*more weird.*"

"What is Universe One?" Raxus asked, turning towards Omega.

"That is where we need to get to," she snapped back, angrily. "And that means the Hybrids still share our goal."

"But they killed Jorge!" Harmony objected.

"And they appear to be in league with the Chronobots, who are definitely not working with us," Raxus added.

"I know," was Omega's irritable response. "And I can only assume that the Hybrids want us dead as well."

"But they still share our goal?" Raxus asked, more confused.

"They can't want the end of all existence any more than us," Omega insisted. "They are trying to get to Universe One to find the root cause of the collapse."

"What is Universe One?" Raxus asked again.

"It is the first simulation, the initial universe that spawned all of these other realities. Somewhere inside it is the original simulation of me, made from the consciousness I downloaded from my universe."

"You are a simulation?" Raxus asked, incredulous.

"We all are. The simulation created simulations of me when I entered the program, replicating different versions through all of the realities it had seeded. We only saw eight others back there, but there are probably an almost infinite number."

"Simulations?" Raxus whispered again, not willing to believe the explanation.

"At least there probably were that many," Omega continued, ignoring his confusion. "As the simulations collapse, we are being reduced further and further. I have a feeling the Chronobots are aiding in that reduction to make the Hybrid's job of finding Universe One that little bit easier. Once all of the other simulations have collapsed, there will only be the original program left."

"So the Universe reduces to one and then expands back out? That doesn't seem so bad?"

Harmony had asked the question, which should have provoked Omega to consider how she was keeping up with the conversation. Instead, she was only slightly impressed on her grasp of the events.

"The original program is not the universe," Omega continued. "The original program is what designs the universe, according to all of the available data it has."

"Its an AI?" Raxus asked, slowly getting over the fact that everything was actually a simulation. Omega placed a hand on his shoulder, emphasising the importance of her next statement:

"It is probably *exactly* like the one your people designed in the final days of your universe. Which is probably what is maintaining the universes we are presently passing through."

"So a civilization like my own created an AI that simulated the known universe, which we are presently within?"

"And that civilization was also a simulation, created by a program I designed," Omega added.

"But you are just a simulation as well?"

"Right. I am a simulated version of the consciousness I downloaded into the program to work out why it was going wrong. The AI created a simulation of my consciousness. That is what I am – within its simulation."

"So what am I?" Harmony asked, looking between the two with the same wide and confused eyes as earlier.

"I think we are just simulations as well," Raxus stated. "And that the entire universe is just a construct?"

"Everything in this universe is at the whim of the AI that formed it," Omega stated. "And I have no control nor knowledge of that AI. It was made by your people – albeit from a different universe, but definitely from your civilization."

"This sounds a lot like the multiverse war," Raxus stated. "The other universes were all warring with us because they found that our universe was the root of all their paradoxes."

"Your universe was one of the stems," Omega continued. "It spawned them in the same way that Universe One spawned your universe. You are all branches from Universe One's tree."

"How far down the chain do you think we are?" Raxus asked, calculating the possible number of universes that could have been created. He rapidly found himself juggling a number in his head some way above infinity. He abandoned that thought quite quickly, as his head span.

"It is impossible to tell," she shook her head. "If we can get back to your Capsule we could use it to travel back to the earliest point in time and wait for the Hybrids to merge dimensions back then. The closer we are to the initial moment of creation, the closer to the root we will be."

"How are we supposed to do that?" Raxus asked. "It was left in the last dimension."

"I assume that the Raxus and Omega that turned up here also had a Capsule?"

"I guess..."

"So we just need to get to it."

"Through a complex filled with psychotic robotic killers?" Harmony asked, terrified. Omega just shrugged.

"Other than the Chronobots, nothing should be able to harm me. Until I can work out what they are trying to do, I refuse to count them as a threat. I remind you – this is just a simulation."

"What about us?" Raxus asked.

"You are a copy I made," she explained. "You should be fine."

"And me?" Harmony asked, wondering if she was also immune in this simulated universe. Omega's expression told her differently.

"Best you stay behind us," she stated, placing a hand on her shoulder. "You humans are quite delicate."

Omega led them out, confidently stepping into the corridor with only the slightest of concern for the Chronobots. The gunfire had receded and there was a calm silence permeating the air.

Making their way back the route they had come, they passed the two halves of the Hybrid that Omega had torn up. Harmony lingered for a moment, staring down into its severed corpse and the mix of fluids that were pooling around it. As she did so, the ground suddenly shifted in multiple places at once, merged with the walls and ceiling and then dropped back down, a few feet from where it had been. All of them lost their balance, scrabbling around in the air with flailing limbs for a moment. Gravity stopped existing and other fundamental laws of reality went into flux. Then they were collapsing in unison as the universe reformed in a slightly different position.

Omega swore in twelve dialects that had never existed in this reality and pulled herself back up to her feet. Raxus did likewise (without swearing), and caught hold of the wall to keep his balance. His head was spinning and it took him a moment to get his eyes to stop swirling with his vision.

Harmony had landed in the severed bottom half of the Hybrid. She was the slowest to recover from the event and pulled herself up out of the squishy mess with increasing disgust. The red and black fluids from its insides (which she was quite sure was a mix of oil and blood) dripped off her knees, cheeks, chin and hands. She screwed her face up, clenched her fists and bottled up the urge to vomit.

"At least we know they are still climbing up the chain," Omega commented, ignoring her predicament. "Every time they do that, we get a little closer."

"It also means they should be distracted," Raxus stated, helping Harmony up whilst trying to ignore the goo dripping from her. She found her feet again and quietly thanked him, meekly looking back at the dormant body. He wiped his hands down and looked back up the corridor.

"Let's take advantage of this lull and get to the surface," he insisted, starting forwards again. Omega fell into step with him, keeping an eye on Harmony as she did so. The confused, dirty and dripping woman dragged her attention from the body and followed them, wiping her hands on her ruined dress.

"I am not sure how much more of this I can take," she stated, looking down at herself. The one thing she had to be grateful for was that she had only thrown on old clothes to go to the shop this morning. Since then, she had been accosted in the supermarket, had her house invaded, been transported several thousand miles in an instant and exposed to some kind of multidimensional war with rampaging, psychotic robot killers and spiked humanoid monstrosities. Now she was watching the innards of one of those monstrosities drip down her legs and roll off her ruined dress in clumps.

"Keep up," Omega demanded, not taking her eyes off the other woman. "We have not got time to dawdle."

"Leave the poor girl alone," Raxus snapped back at her. "You have shown little to no compassion since you turned up!"

Before she could respond, they rounded the corner and entered the corridor leading down to the control room. Three Hybrids stood in their path, all of which turned in eerie unison towards them. Standing next to them, however, was the Director – Professor Abrienne.

"You're dead!" Harmony exclaimed, failing to notice the Hybrids' spikes flick towards them.

"Get back," Omega warned, shoving her backwards. Raxus fell back around the corner with her, hastily getting out of view of the Hybrids and their spiked armaments. A moment later there was a flurry of sharp projectiles in the air where his face had been, just missing him.

Omega stepped into the full blast, catching the spikes in her open arms and across her chest. The few that might have managed to hit Harmony and Raxus struck her instead, penetrating her flesh in three dozen places.

Every single one of the projectiles slid off her, without leaving a mark. It was as if her flesh simply rejected them, popping them out and dropping them onto the floor like discarded matchsticks.

She marched straight up to the closest of the Hybrids. The Director, backing away in a similar way to how Raxus had, almost fell over as she took hold of the creature. Ignoring the spikes that cut through her hands, she dug her fingers into the shoulder blades. Securing her grip as the other two creatures attempted to grab hold of her, she then yanked in opposite directions.

The Hybrid was torn into two pieces, its innards spraying out in a blackish, reddish hue. It made an ungodly noise as its flesh and wiring tore and then went limp, dropping from her hands with a split from shoulder to navel.

The other two piled onto her, attempting to topple her over. Finding her like a rock, they heaved this way and that without success. Instead, she took hold of one of their arms and (to their great surprise) began heaving it off of her and into the air. The other one attempted to take out her legs, kicking at her knees to try and buckle her over.

"Raxus!" she shouted round the corner – realising that he was not helping. "Get out here!"

His head appeared at the edge of the corridor, peeking around the corner at her and the two remaining Hybrids. By now she had lifted one off the floor completely, dangling it by its arm while the other repeatedly kicked at the back of her knee.

"Help me!" she shouted at him. The Hybrid kicking at her leg turned towards him, its spikes regenerating in a flash and firing out in his direction. He ducked back behind the corner, the bolts narrowly missing him.

Omega despaired with him and swung the Hybrid she was holding at the other one. Using it as a flail, she knocked the creature away from her and stopped it from pursuing Raxus around the corner. The one in her grasp went limp and she swung it again, whipping it up around her head to bring its body smashing down on the other one. When they connected, both carapaces cracked as if they were eggs being knocked together. They went limp and Omega dropped the creature to the floor.

The Director stared at her and the three bodies.

"What the hell is going on?" he asked, staring in terror. "Are you here to kill me?"

"You?" Omega asked, swinging towards him. "No. Why would I want to?"

"I saw you die..." Harmony declared, quietly from the corner. Omega grimaced and shook her head.

"You saw a previous root dimension's simulation of him," she explained, peevishly. "I am curious as to whether we will see another simulation of you here..."

Abrienne took the opportunity to bolt back into the control room, throwing the door open and diving inside. He was replaced by the Hybrid they had seen earlier, who was now active and stepping up into the corridor. Its spikes arrowed towards Omega.

She ignored them and stepped forwards, letting the bolts spatter across her and then drop off, harmlessly.

"You and I need to talk," she pointed at the creature. It fired again, sending another barrage of spikes reeling through her. Again, they splattered through her and then dropped harmlessly to the ground.

"We can do this all day."

It fired again, failing to slow her advance.

"I don't want to stop what you are doing here," she continued. "But if you keep getting in my way, I will have no choice."

It fired again, backing inside the room. A number of terrified faces flickered around behind it, attempting to get a view of the impossibly invulnerable woman that was marching towards them. Abrienne was shouting something that Omega could not hear.

"Just keep doing what you are doing," she insisted, walking right up to the door and into the face of the creature. It backed away further, now fully inside the room.

Omega reached inside, took hold of the door handle and closed it, locking the hybrid inside. Snapping it off, she then smiled to herself.

"There," she declared. "That should solve that problem."

The door exploded from the inside as the Hybrid applied its many weapons against it, shattering the frame and structure in a burst of concentrated plasma. Standing in the forefront of the eruption, Omega was caught by the burst of flame and winced as its heat and fire flickered over her. It did not affect her - other than causing a slightly more peeved expression to cross her face.

"Will you never learn?" she asked, turning towards the now shattered doorway. The Hybrid fired again, sending a torrent of spikes through the smoking hole and into her. She ignored them and instead took a step backwards, looking up at the smoking, cracked arch of the doorway. As the Hybrid regenerated its spikes to fire again, she reached up and took hold of the broken frame. With one good heave (ignoring another spray of spikes from the Hybrid), she tore out the supporting lintel. The doorway collapsed, sealing the room with an increasing avalanche of masonry.

"Lets try that again, shall we?" Omega asked – chastising herself for thinking that the door would have held them.

"You just sealed them in there?" Raxus asked. "How long will that keep them?"

"Long enough for us to get to the surface. I hope," Omega replied. "Come on."

She marched down the corridor, heading towards the lift that Jorge had used to bring them down.

Harmony followed, picking her way past the three Hybrid corpses whilst trying not to look at them. Their oil and blood was pooling out over the floor, making it increasingly treacherous to walk through. She tried her best to get through without stepping in it, succeeding in only staining the tips of her shoes. Omega seemed not to worry, as neither the oil nor blood seemed to stain her – in the same way that the Hybrid's shards had not affected her. They all just seemed to slide off her, as if nothing could gain a purchase.

They reached the lift without further interruption, giving little more than a worried glance back the way they came. There was no sign of any kind of pursuit. The lift was already on its way down to them and they had to wait a precious few more moments in silence as it rattled down into view.

They immediately spotted the assortment of legs and bodies occupying the elevator. All three started to back away. A moment later,

Raxus, Jorge and Omega were staring out through the mesh wire door back at them.

"Ah, the product of the latest foray?" Omega asked, before the lift finished rattling to a stop. Jorge just looked confused at her and then back at the other Omega, in the lift with him.

"What are you?" the other Omega (Omega[b]) asked, stepping up to haul the lift door open.

"You are a simulated product of the AI that created this universe," our Omega snapped at her, marching up to meet her. "We are cutting things short because we are about twenty minutes or so ahead of you in your timeline. We need to use the Capsule you used to get here."

"Its back on the surface," Raxus[b] replied, also stepping past an increasingly confused looking Jorge.

"Don't tell them anything," Omega[b] snapped at him. "We still aren't clear on who they are."

"We are simulated versions of a branch reality," Omega sighed, stepping past her to get to the lift. "Our universe has already collapsed – probably entirely at this point. There are a group of Hybrids here that are climbing the chain back towards the root reality that spawned this version of the simulation."

"The AI you were talking about?" Omega[b] swung back towards her Raxus. He just looked blankly between them all.

"Harmony?" Jorge asked, finally spotting her. She looked relieved at seeing him alive, but quickly changed to concern as he held out a hand towards her.

"What are you doing here?" he asked, increasingly frantic. "Who are these people? What are they doing here? Nobody should be in the complex!"

"You did not encounter her?" Omega asked, waiting inside the lift for the other two. Jorge had stopped Harmony at the entrance, holding her shoulder as she had tried to follow Raxus inside.

"Who is she?" Omega[b] asked.

The conversation ended when a sharp flash interrupted them. At its epicentre was a rapidly materialising sequence of cogs, wheels, wires and metal. Everyone except Jorge recognised the unmistakeable materialisation of one of the Chronobots.

Omega grabbed Harmony and yanked her from Jorge's grip, dragging her inside the lift with a tug that almost dislocated her shoulder. She yelped and dragged Jorge along with her, pulling him half inside the lift and blocking the door.

The Chronobot finished materialising and raised its arm, pointing towards Omega[b], who stood arrogantly assuming that she was still completely invulnerable to everything within her simulation. Omega considered warning her, but was more preoccupied with Jorge – blocking the lift doorway and preventing her escape.

Omega[b] disintegrated. The smug, arrogant expression faded from her face as her body dissolved. Raxus[b] yelped and tried to lunge for the lift. Omega shoved Jorge out of the door and into him, stopping him in his tracks and directly in front of the Chronobot. She then hauled the lift door closed and hammered for the ascend button. It did so with a disturbingly calm and slow pace.

The Chronobot shifted its attention to Raxus[b] and a moment later he was also fading from existence. Where he and Jorge had once been entangled at the door, Jorge was now suddenly alone and facing the Chronobot. The lift slowly rattled upwards, with all three of its occupants crouching down to see through the bottom of its mesh door.

The Chronobot disappeared again, leaving Jorge alone in the corridor. The lift rattled the last few feet upwards, robbing its occupants of seeing any further.

"What just happened?" Raxus asked.

"Is he okay down there?" Harmony asked. "I mean... Jorge? Will he be okay?"

"Both of these are very good questions," Omega grumbled. "I can only assume that there is currently only one Jorge in this reality and that therefore he is not a threat to paradox. At the moment."

"As soon as they shift again, the Chronobots will start hunting us again?" Raxus asked.

"It seems they do not particularly care which version of us survives – so long as there is only one left in each reality."

"Which makes sense – given their aversion to paradox," Raxus nodded, at least understanding a little of what was happening around him. "Why aren't they stopping the Hybrids, though? They are the ones causing the paradoxes."

"They can't want all reality to collapse," Omega affirmed once more. "Nobody wants that."

"Then surely they know that we are here to help?" Raxus asked. "Why eliminate us?"

"We still don't know the root cause of the collapse," Omega sighed. "Whatever is causing the collapse may have a vested interest in stopping us."

"You are suggesting a malevolent force behind it?!" he exclaimed. "What kind of intelligence would want to end all of existence?!"

The lift suddenly faded out of reality, shifting itself into the open drop of the shaft below it. The floors, walls and ceiling seemed to blur into a mesh of one another, as if three dimensions had temporarily become one.

For a moment they feared that the collapse had reached them – that this was the final death of reality.

It was over in a heartbeat and when their vision reaffirmed that reality was behaving normally again, they found they were on the floor of the lift. It rattled to a halt at the top of the shaft and came to rest.

"We just shifted again," Raxus stated the obvious.

"Which means there will be more of us again," Omega added. "Which means the Chronobots are hunting us again. Stay alert."

Chapter Twelve

Dimensional Parley

They emerged from the lift, still slightly confused by the shift in reality. Even though they had only been there a short time before, everything appeared to be the wrong way around – as if the room had been laid out as a mirror image of how they remembered it.

"Isn't the entrance that way?" Raxus asked, staring at the blank metal wall at the far end. Harmony was stood next to him, still trying to get her head around the fact that everything was backwards. Omega, swiftly adjusting to the new reality, marched across the open floor towards the clearly marked exit. The inverted writing over the door made no difference to her – she could read it just as easily forwards as backwards.

The door had been electronically sealed again. Recalling what Jorge had done to open it earlier, Raxus bent down to examine the system. It promptly swung open, while he was still looking, revealing Jorge standing there. He almost leapt back in surprise.

"What are you doing here?" he demanded.

Omega held up her hands and pushed her way out past him, into the sunlight.

"Thank you," she smiled, as she passed. He stared at Harmony.

"What are you doing here?!" he exclaimed, with even more surprise.

"I am not entirely sure," she replied, sheepishly.

"I thought you were back in England?" he asked. "Your project got closed down?"

"It did. I was. I think you better come with us," she tried to explain. "These guys seem to know more about it all than I do."

"Who are they? What were you doing in the facility?"

By this point both Raxus and Omega were headed across the gravel car park and passed his parked vehicle. Following them, Jorge and Harmony continued their discussion. Then they stopped and stared across the open road and at the empty field, opposite.

"Its not there," Omega stated. Ahead was the road that led into the car park, the dilapidated hut and a large open field of sunflowers. There was no sign of the large, monolithic black capsule.

"I can see that," Raxus replied, irritably. "We have shifted quite a few realities since we left it here."

"Shouldn't there be another one? From this reality?"

"We can't be sure what will be in any of the realities we phase into," Raxus stated. "We are hopping dimensions – we might not even exist in this world. Almost anything is possible."

"I can't believe that," Omega shook her head. "I am in every reality. That blob and gas version of myself convinced me of that. It has made me a fundamental part of every simulation."

"So... by extension I am as well?" he asked.

"And therefore the capsule is also," she confirmed.

As if summoned by her affirmation, a black monolith promptly plopped into existence in the middle of the sunflower field, sticking out in exactly the way a large black monolith would.

"Our carriage," she smiled, confidently.

Emerging from the inky black stone came Raxus[d] and Omega[d]. Harmony was again suspiciously absent from their group, causing Omega to slow and reappraise the pair. In turn, the newcomers stopped a few steps from the monolith and stared at them. It did not escape their attention that their opposite number appeared almost completely their opposite this time – with their faces mirrored. Where Raxus had his fringe cutting over the right of his brow, Raxus[d] had his over his left.

"That's close enough," Omega[d] warned. "Who and what are you?"

"We are quite obviously you," Omega snapped – as if she was irritated with herself. "We have just hopped into your reality and now we are looking to leave it. We have not got much time before the Chronobots turn up. This paradoxical situation is bound to attract them."

She waved her hand between the two versions of herself, emphasising the point.

"Now let us inside the Capsule and we will be on our way."

"Now there are four of them?" Jorge asked, staring between the duplicates of Omega and Raxus.

"There were two more of you as well," Harmony replied. "God knows how many of them there have been."

"Which is a point," Omega swung round towards her. Pointing a finger at the now startled woman, she continued (accusingly); "Where is your version of her?"

"Who is she?" Omega[d] asked, staring at the woman as if she had never seen her before her in her life.

"A good question. If we had our bracelets working we could find out immediately."

She stepped up towards Harmony as she spoke, looking over the woman as if she was dissecting her with her eyes.

"Where did you just come from?" Raxus asked, stepping up to intercede and prevent Omega from terrifying the woman.

"We had to bounce around the year fourteen billion, to avoid the paradox events there," Raxus[d] explained. "We almost didn't make it at all."

"See," Raxus held up a hand to Omega. "They did not take the same route as us. Therefore they never picked her up."

"So why did we?" Omega demanded. "What makes her so special that she only got picked up in our universe?"

"We don't know that," he countered. "We just haven't come across another one yet. There are probably infinite possibilities – you said it yourself."

"I can still be suspicious."

"So can I. You still need to explain yourselves," Omega[d] demanded. Omega sighed.

"We really do not have the time. We are creating a paradox being here. Raxus knows what that means."

"She might have a point," Raxus[d] commented, quietly. "If there are Chronobots active in this area-"

"The Chronobots are not a threat," Omega[d] cut him off, arrogantly. Omega considered warning her that her immortality did not extend to the Chronobots' powers, but decided against it when one materialised in front of them.

"Conversation is over," she stated, pushing past her opposite number. The creature finished its materialisation before she got two steps and was immediately raising its mechanical, clockwork arm.

Omega[d] grabbed her as she pushed her, stopping her advance and swinging her around. Seeing the Chronobot raising its arm towards both of them, Omega heartlessly shoved her doppelgänger in front. She promptly disintegrated in her arms, fading from existence.

Raxus did not hesitate and pushed passed them both, ignoring the surprised yelp as Omega[d] disappeared. Grabbing Harmony by the hand, he hauled her inside the capsule without looking back. They slipped through the inky black stone and emerged on the other side, within the safety of the control room.

Omega staggered backwards as her double disappeared but stopped as she reached the edge of the capsule. The Chronobot shifted its attention to Raxus[d] and he also promptly faded from existence. Placing a hand out on the edge of the capsule, Omega waited for a heartbeat to pass to see what it would do next.

Raxus activated the exterior monitor from within the capsule, staring at the events as they unfolded.

Jorge stood rooted to the spot, staring at the clockwork creature.

The sunflowers waved in the breeze.

It disappeared.

There was a moment of silence as the wind gently ruffled its way through the field.

"Its mission was accomplished, I guess," Omega stated, mainly to herself.

Then six Hybrids opened fire from the dilapidated hut. A shower of shards rained across the field, slicing the heads off the sunflowers and peppering the ground. They fell from Omega like rain, harmlessly splashing across her front. Jorge was not so blessed. His body was lacerated with a dozen different hits, the shards eating through his body in a wave. His head was severed from his shoulders and dropped to the ground at his feet. A moment later his knees buckled and his body crumpled, following it down.

Harmony gasped from within the capsule, protected inside its shell but traumatised at seeing her friend killed for the second time that day. Raxus continued to watch the projection, curious as to what Omega was doing.

Omega stepped forwards, confidently keeping her back to the capsule. Jorge's body rolled to a stop next to her. The Hybrids responded with another wave of spikes, raining across the field like thousands of arrowheads.

"Okay, now we have been reduced to one copy again, maybe we can start talking?" she asked. The spikes dropped from her harmlessly, leaving several severed sunflowers in their wake.

"Your Chronobot friends have left and you can't hurt me. Whatever intelligence is controlling you must have some questions. Let's talk."

The six Hybrids stopped regenerating their spikes.

"Good," she smiled, stepping towards them. "We appear to be making progress."

"Threat analysis confirmed. You are the Omega."

"You know my name. That's a good start," she continued towards them. "Can you explain why you keep killing everyone around you?"

"Complete assimilation of resources is paramount for survival. All opposing or irrelevant organics must be eliminated to reduce factors."

The statement made a surprising amount of sense to Omega, who cared little for the blood letting (as everyone they killed was merely a simulation, anyway).

"So each time you hop universes you reduce everything back down to manageable numbers? So you don't end up with multiple timelines again?"

"Omega's analysis is correct."

"So would I be right in assuming that you are already reducing each universe from the initial moment of creation?"

"The moment of creation is a singularity. It is inaccessible. We have created our own singularity in conjunction with it, in order to monitor the collapse and access further root dimensions."

"How close are you to getting to the original root?"

"Information of that nature is not accessible in this time period."

"So I need to get back there to find out?" she asked, largely to herself. Looking back at the capsule in the field, she shrugged and started to head back to it. "That seems easy enough."

Turning back towards the six Hybrids, she called to them; "keep doing what you are doing. It is helping."

She regretted those words as soon as she stepped through the inky stone entrance of the capsule.

"They killed Jorge!" Harmony yelled at her, pointing wildly into the holographic projection. It showed the severed heads of the sunflowers. And it showed Jorge's body, likewise decapitated, alongside them.

"You didn't need to encourage their killing spree," Raxus added, sourly.

"Just set us on a course into the vortex," Omega replied, flippantly. "We need to get as close as possible to year zero."

"Are you on their side now?" Harmony asked, stepping up to her to try and demand an answer. "They killed Jorge!" she repeated.

"We all have the same goal," Omega sighed, stepping around her. "None of us wants existence to end. Raxus, set the course for year zero."

"If we get that close to the singularity we will not be able to get away again," Raxus warned her. "We could get dragged in and absorbed into the explosion."

"I know that," Omega snapped. "Get us as close as possible."

"Are you talking about what I think you are talking about?" Harmony interrupted. "The Big Bang?"

"The Hybrids are reducing reality from that point," Omega explained. "Sooner or later it will be the only part of this reality that still exists. At which point they should be able to work out where Universe One is."

"And that is a good thing?" Harmony asked, worriedly. "All of the other universes being destroyed?"

"If it means we can get to Universe One, then yes. Only one universe is needed, for one thing."

"I beg to differ," Raxus interrupted. "If time travel is to exist then multiple dimensions are fundamental."

"Time travel should not exist," Omega snapped. "All of this is wrong. Physics should only allow time to travel in one direction;

forwards. Bending it back like this is part of the reason this simulation is going wrong."

"If it is all just a simulation then time travel has to be possible," Raxus shot back at her. "Otherwise the simulation wouldn't have any past or future written for the program to run from."

Omega was about to argue back when she realised that he had answered part of the fundamental problem for her. She had never considered that time travel would have to exist within her simulation – as it did not exist within the 'real world'.

He had solved it for her. She had to get back to her reality and program in parameters that allowed for time travel. This would stop the uncontrollable paradox effect that was feeding the collapse.

Now all that remained was finding out what (or who) was triggering the collapse.

"Raxus Pross, you are quite possibly the most important being in all realities," she beamed at him. "I can see why you were so important that I had to bring you with me. Now set a course for year zero."

"I love the fact that you think so highly of me," he began tampering with the controls, "but you are still asking for us all to leap to our deaths by doing this."

"We are flying into the Big Bang?" Harmony repeated, trying her best to keep up with the conversation.

"Is that really what your people call it?" Omega asked, exasperated with her interruptions. Considering it was the most remarkable event in existence, the human term for it seemed painfully simple. For one thing, the bang was actually infinitesimally small – considering the universe began at a microscopic size. The explosion did continue for some time (in a manner of speaking, it can be argued to still be continuing, even in Omega's era) and by the time it had cooled enough to be distinguishable from a huge plasma-like soup of radioactive particles, it was quite big. The term 'Event One' had become more widely used by Raxus's era.

It was the edge of that era that they were aiming for – at a point when matter was just starting to form and the general temperature of the universe was starting to cool enough for atoms to form. There would be no planets, stars nor other stellar objects – only the rapidly forming clouds of hydrogen, helium and lithium - just starting to collapse into one another through gravity.

Omega did not elaborate on any of this and instead waited to see if Harmony was going to answer her patronising question.

"It was a big bang," she stated, quietly in defence of the term. Omega shook her head.

"The course is set," Raxus interrupted them. "Are you sure you want to do this?"

"We have pretty much been given an invitation by the Hybrids," Omega declared. "It would be rude to turn it down at this point."

"Or they have come up with a different way of trying to kill you?" Raxus suggested. "Their weapons don't work – so they send you back to the biggest explosion in history?"

"See - 'Big' ..." Harmony added, to continue defending the human term.

"You really don't trust them?" Omega asked him, ignoring her entirely.

"No," he replied, steadfast. "And if you knew half of the things they have done, you would not either."

"They do appear a little trigger happy," Omega conceded. "But we all want the same thing. They just appear to be willing to clear the chaff without moral hesitation."

"A moral hesitation that you appear to be lacking as well," Raxus pointed out, coldly. "Do you even care about all the deaths back there?"

"They are all simulations," Omega sighed. "We are all simulations. There is a root universe out there somewhere and maybe I will care about individuals in that one. At the moment I care about you, Raxus, as you have been invaluable. I also care about Harmony, as she continues to be an enigma to me."

"An enigma?" she cut in, wondering if that was a compliment.

"Now set the course," Omega insisted, continuing to ignore her.

"I don't want to consign myself to death at the heart of creation," he replied, forcefully. "I don't trust the Hybrids and I don't think I should trust you."

"Do you have a choice?" Omega countered, folding her arms.

"What do you mean?"

"This universe is collapsing, just like all the others. At some point that collapse will reach here and everything will cease to exist. If you don't use the capsule to go further back, you will also get swallowed in the collapse. And then how far back do you go? It will chase you back down the vortex until... until you reach the initial moment of creation. And then - one way or another, you are destroyed and the universe never existed in first place."

As she had spoken, she had stepped around him, surveying the controls in a desperate bid to work out how the system functioned. As her speech had continued, she had steadily realised that she had no idea about how temporal mechanics would work as it was as far from her reality as science fiction was from actual physics. There were panels, screens, dials and rows of buttons but no clear description of what any of them did. By the time she reached the last sentence of her soliloquy, she had come to the decision that she was going to have to continue to depend on Raxus to get it moving.

"I see your point," he conceded (much to her relief). Pressing down onto the controls, he activated the capsule and guided them back through time.

The black block of monolithic stone wobbled once and then flopped out of the field and into the time vortex, leaving behind it a scattering of severed sunflowers and Jorge's decapitated body. The Hybrids returned to their task – steadily eating their way through realities as each dimension crumbled and collapsed in their wake.

The time stream looked worse than before and Raxus spent a few moments making sure they weren't about to drop headlong into the collapse. Ripples and fluctuations were reaching all through the vortex, concentrating around events and people that no longer existed. Much of the future had disappeared.

The capsule dropped through this storm like a sparrow trapped in a crosswind, buffeted by the turbulent waves and thrown like jetsam across its depths. He struggled at the controls, wrestling to keep them on a steady course whilst avoiding the paradox eddies forming all around them. Where the time stream had once been filled with other travellers, it was now awash with ghosts of their travels – leaving dangerous trenches where they had once trod.

"Can you keep this thing steady?" Omega complained, taking hold of the console to balance herself. Raxus pushed past her, concentrating on avoiding crashing them into a paradox. Harmony was sprawled on the seat, grasping at the cushions whilst staring wild eyed at them both.

The Capsule leapt one last time and then steadied, emerging from the turbulence as suddenly as it had entered. For a moment Raxus had to make sure they were still in flight and hadn't crashed into an unwanted time zone.

"Well done," Omega complimented him. Straightening herself from her position over the console, she brushed herself down and smiled. He just shook his head at her.

"That had nothing to do with me," he stated. "The vortex suddenly calmed itself. Something is going on out there."

"What do you mean?" Omega asked, drawing herself over the console – as if she could understand what it was telling them.

"Someone is maintaining the vortex out there," Raxus explained. "They have eliminated the paradox effects."

"The Hybrids?"

"This is beyond their capabilities..." he shook his head. "Even my civilization at its peak would have difficulty doing this..."

"Your civilization no longer exists," Omega pointed out, heartlessly. "Any other suggestions?"

"There are not that many civilizations that could harness time travel early enough to still exist," he shook his head. "The first civilizations were very war-like and wiped each other out before they had a chance."

"Some things appear to be universal. All of the first races wiped themselves out before my era."

"We are approaching the zero point," Raxus warned. "We are going to have to materialize soon."

"How close can you get us?"

"The vortex still appears unnaturally smooth here," he shrugged. "I have no idea if it is going to just suddenly give out when we hit zero."

"Bring us out now," Omega shrugged. "We should be able to see what they are doing to maintain the area."

Raxus flipped a switch and looked up at the holographic projection. The image settled into a blurred, hazy mess of warm colours and flickers of light. There were no distinguishable shapes and no sign of any kind of life or structures. Hydrogen, helium and lithium swam around them in clouds of cooling gas, steadily condensing towards the first stars.

"I think we landed around eight million years from the zero point," Raxus explained. "There is no sign of any kind of life or matter out there yet."

"Then what is that?" Harmony asked, pointing to the image. Swimming through the cloud, as if it was basking in their oddly warm coloured waters, was some kind of creature. It had at least a dozen spindly legs, wriggling like tentacles. They protruded from a huge, bulbous body with a small, fat head at one end.

"That is a Magua," Raxus declared, surprised and enthused. "I never knew they could do that!"

"Indeed it is!" Omega beamed, happily. She was more overjoyed to see the result of her programming skills than she was about the fact that it was there. She had already seen one, far in the future and back on the Temporal Station. Seeing one here, in its natural environment, was a reward she hadn't considered.

"Its coming towards us," Harmony pointed out. Omega shook off the sense of awe the creature imbibed in her and looked over at Raxus.

"It can't do anything to us, can it?" she asked. "We are safe in here, aren't we?"

The early Magua were a notoriously violent species. Being the first creature to occupy the universe, they had a significant head start on all of the other races that evolved in their wake. Consequently, they were known in Omega's reality for attempting to wipe out all other life before it could evolve into a threat against them. This tactic largely worked – reducing the number of early races significantly. Eventually they were toppled and another race took the helm, hunting all other less evolved races before they could become a threat to them. This cycle continued for some time, until the various species that inhabited the universe realised that their time and number were limited.

None of this is relevant here, as the simulated universe took a significantly different path. The Magua were not wiped out and instead managed to crack time travel before anyone else had the opportunity. They spread all the way through time, becoming the longest surviving species in the universe and a guiding force within the time war.

This was now very much to their benefit, as all of the other time travelling species were now wiped out – having been deleted by the collapsing simulation.

They thought they had won the time war.

Until their capsule arrived.

The Celestials and Magua had maintained an agreement to avoid each other's sensitive time zones. In the early moments of the time war they had both initiated rather crude and devastating attacks on each other. The Celestials had attempted to prevent the Magua from evolving. The Magua attempted to wipe out all life in the universe at the very first moments of creation. Both attempts caused a paradox that very nearly ended existence. Only the intervention of Chronobots, Hybrids and other paradoxical elements of the time war prevented it.

The result of this chaos had been a peace treaty between almost all sides. They agreed not to cause any other universe-ending paradoxes and avoid entering each other's sensitive eras. This era – so close to the birth of the universe – was deemed one of those sensitive eras.

The Magua launched itself onto their monolith and wrapped its many limbs around its cold, black stone. Hugging it close to its huge, obese body, it then seemed to wriggle its way up through the clouds, dragging them along with it.

"What is it doing?" Omega asked. Raxus just checked the console, making sure he was reading it correctly.

"We are immobilized," he stated, throwing a few of the switches and hammering a dial. The hologram over their heads showed the huge beast wrapped around them, its spindly legs so close over the camera that they could make out the razor-like hairs on them.

"Where is it taking us?" Omega asked, noting the fact that they were being dragged quite quickly in one direction.

"Your guess is as good as mine," Raxus sighed, giving up with controls. "There shouldn't be anything out there. No planets, no stars, nothing."

"Can it time travel?" she continued, examining it through the hologram.

"I am guessing it does," he shrugged. "It shouldn't have had time to evolve in this period. It must have come back from a later era. One that still exists."

"Along with those others?" Harmony asked from her seat. She was pointing up into the projection, past the creature that was wrapped around them. Beyond it were thousands of the creatures, emerging from the gas in waves and seemingly swimming through the balmy depths like a school of fish. They were all headed in one direction, appearing like salmon headed upstream. Many were carrying or dragging things along with them – none of which were distinguishable at this distance.

Raxus checked their course on the controls and confirmed his fears.

"There is some kind of huge structure," he stated. "Made from materials that shouldn't exist yet..."

"Can you shift our view?" Omega asked, waving her hand at the projection. Raxus obliged and a moment later the station came rolling into view. It looked much like any other deep space outpost to them. For Harmony it was spectacular – reaching out through the warm clouds with huge, spindly antennae and docking platforms. To Raxus and Omega, it seemed quite crude – made up of technologies salvaged from the earliest eras of existence.

The flock of creatures seemed to be descending towards it, spiralling in from the clouds in indistinguishable lines. There were so many that it was difficult to discern one from the next, as their shapes and shadows merged with the clouds.

"It is surrounded by Chronobots," Omega warned. For a moment the other two just continued to stare into the projection, mesmerised. Then they began to make out the differences between the tiny flecks, spiralling around the station. Many of them were not Magua at all. Many of them were the unmistakeable clockwork metal of the Chronobots.

"What are they doing here?" Raxus asked, staring in fear at the projection.

"They don't appear to be doing anything," she continued. They hung around the immense station like flies, whilst the Magua seemed to be funnelling into it.

"Its almost like they are guarding the entrance," she added, taking a step around the projection.

"We are following them in," Raxus warned – the hologram showed the station rapidly growing in the foreground. The creature wrapped around their exterior showed no sign of slowing.

"Some of those are ships," Harmony added, pointing deeper into the projection. Now that they were closer, they could make out that the Magua were dragging in other craft. One looked like a classic Saturn Five rocket from Earth, hauled towards the station by a pair of huge, bloated Magua.

The massive station loomed over the image and blocked their view of the clouds. The creature that was wrapped around them finally let go and suddenly they found themselves at rest, on the surface of the station and surrounded by other craft and confused looking creatures. There were three other ships directly in their view, all of different designs and sizes. One was almost as small as their capsule, whilst another was about three hundred meters long. From the arrangement of beings that were emerging from them, there were at least a dozen humans – all as perplexed looking as themselves.

"Lets go say hello," Omega suggested, stepping towards the capsule door. Raxus followed whilst Harmony remained staring into the hologram and the array of life and technology outside the door. Her day was not likely to get any less strange at this point.

Chapter Thirteen

The Restaurant at the Start of the Universe

It was not so much a restaurant as a collection of food stalls on the edge of the landing pad. The 'Big Bang Burger Bar' would be a more appropriate name.

Dozens of Magua sat behind large open trays of food and barrels of drink. As each creature approached them, they were offered a tray of whatever nutrients were there. It was difficult to discern them, as they all appeared to have the same jelly like texture – even the drinks stored in the barrels. The main difference was in their shocking bright colours – lining the trays in rainbow patterns. The Magua slopped them out like strange, bloated dinner ladies. The aliens likewise seemed to take the trays like obedient school children, none seeming to question the surreality of these magnificent, ancient beings handing out refreshments.

Omega ignored the food vendors and headed through the throng of aliens as they continued to disgorge around her. There were close to a thousand already on the platform, with more appearing all the time. Streams of Magua continued to descend from the sky, depositing more ships onto the platform before moving away again. Some appeared to be ushering them forwards or creating lines. Others, as already noted, were serving food and drinks to the newcomers. There seemed to be soothing music in the air, made of a hundred choir-like voices in harmony. It made the pleasant smell from the food all the more alluring, even if their appearance was slimy and off-putting.

Raxus ignored all of this and followed Omega through the crowds. He was making out dozens of races from all over the time stream – some from almost comparable civilizations to his own. They had already spotted a small group of humans in the throng, though they had been easily lost once they moved into the crowd.

Several groups had started to mingle, creating throngs that were steadily being ushered in towards the food stalls. Omega and Raxus cut their way through these, interrupting a few conversations as they did so. Harmony remained within the relative safety of the Capsule, transfixed by the holographic projection but not willing to risk stepping outside. She had never seen an alien before that day and witnessing the myriad of creatures there had dissuaded her from venturing out. Instead, she began examining each of them from a distance, marvelling at the variety of life outside. We shall gloss over her reactions to the marvellous array of intelligent life for reasons that will become apparent in the subsequent chapter.

"More humans!" a voice cut out from the crowds. Picking it out from between a pair of muscular Endorgs, Omega made out a small group of men and women. One of them was stepping forwards to meet them, a confident and friendly smile on his face. Omega theorised that the soothing psychic singing she could hear was having a strong effect on him.

"Captain James Khan," he introduced himself, his hand outstretched. Omega took it with a wry smile, allowing him to shake it, warmly.

"We are Space Force," he continued, evidently proud of his title, "Captain of the Explorer Class vessel; the *Franchise*. It is good to see other humans. We were starting to worry that we were going to be alone out here."

"Do you know what is going on?" she asked, releasing his hand when it felt natural. The rest of (what she assumed were) his crew congregated behind him. They were all dressed in the same dull grey jumpsuits, with an insignia flecked over the shoulder – probably representing the organisation they worked for. From her understanding of Earth history, they were from Harmony's era.

He likewise took in her and Raxus's dress and assumed they were also in uniform.

"No idea," he answered, flippantly. "Who do you work for, anyway? You haven't got any flags?"

"Flags?" Raxus asked, looking at himself for a moment as he wondered what he meant. Omega's immense intellect was far quicker at interpreting his vernacular and identified the quaint custom of adorning heraldry and nationalist badges. She shook her head.

"We are independents," she summarised, in a way he would understand.

"Well its good to see something else as beautiful as the view," Khan beamed at her. He stepped a little closer, as if to put himself between her and Raxus. "Are you two a research couple?"

"Not exactly," Raxus interceded.

"Are you a couple?" he continued, keeping his gaze on Omega and ignoring Raxus entirely.

"No," was her cold response. She could tell from his elevated testosterone levels and dilated pupils that he was interested in the organic recepticle she had simulated. Having absolutely no interest in his sexuality and fully aware of the number of testosterone imbued captains that humanity promulgated, she rapidly started to lose interest in him and his group.

"Do you know why we were brought here?" he asked, without picking up on her coldness.

"No," she smiled, icily. She had hoped he had been briefed by the Magua as to what they were doing there. His ignorance made her immediately lose interest entirely and she began looking through the crowd for a more enlightened creature. The Magua were all zipping in and out too fast for her to catch. For one thing, she would like to question them about the soothing psychic singing she could feel pressing on her brain: They were trying to keep everyone pacified.

The Endorgs she had spotted earlier were one of the elder races – long extinct before her time. Even if it did not have any answers, she could at least enjoy herself by talking to a creature she would never have had a chance to talk to.

She turned her back on them and walked away without another word.

"Excuse me?" Khan exclaimed, surprised and clearly offended by her disregard.

"Sorry about her," Raxus apologised. "She's like that."

"She never answered my question," he frowned, finally turning to him. "Who are you?"

"My apologies, Captain Khan. It was Space Force you were part of, right?" he asked, checking his Earth history as he spoke. Khan nodded.

"As I recall, you were engaged in the exploration of near solar objects? What are you doing back here?"

"One of those creatures dragged us off course," Khan explained. "We were a few hundred klicks off Eris when it hit us. We thought it was another asteroid in the Kuiper Belt, something we had missed. Then this creature... the Magua... latched onto us. It hauled us at some impossible speed into this nebula. We have never seen anything like it."

Raxus looked between the crew as the captain recounted their story, slightly amazed at their experience. They were clearly from an early exploration team, right on the edges of their solar system. The Magua must have dragged them from their time period to here, in some kind of an attempt at rescuing them from the imminent collapse of their timeline.

Rather than try and explain any of this to them, he just shrugged and continued:

"We had a similar experience. You have no idea where you are now?"

"None," the captain shook his head, smiling inanely as he looked around. There was something about how he was taking it all in his stride that unnerved him. In fact, there had to be hundreds of alien species all gathering on the platform – all of them seemed unusually at ease with the situation.

This led Raxus to draw the next question out a little slower, testing how much they were ready to understand.

"Or when you are?" he asked, carefully.

"What do you mean?"

He cleared his throat, bracing himself for the long explanation ahead. He had only just got his head around the fact that he was a simulation. He had his doubts that this youthful band of explorers were going to find it so easy.

"I think you and your crew had better brace yourselves. You have not just travelled through space."

"What do you mean?" he asked again, a little more strongly.

"We are from the far future," he tried to explain, sounding more apologetic with each syllable. "We are trying to stop the universe from collapsing and we think the Magua are trying to help."

This led to the inevitable long explanation from Raxus, which culminated with his attempt at describing how they were all just simulations within a simulated universe that had been simulated by an artificial intelligence for an entirely different universe. This did not earn him much sympathy from the captain and his crew. In fact, Khan seemed more interested in pursuing Omega than he was with his explanation.

"So your lady friend is single?" he pressed, ignoring the rest of his crew as several started rolling their eyes.

"I am not entirely sure you can describe her as a lady..." was his honest, but quiet reply.

"She certainly looks like a lady to me. A real lady," was the distracted comment that came back. The Captain was starting to scan the crowd again, with a wistful and lustful look in his eye.

"We appear to be being directed this way, captain," his first officer commented. The line was indeed starting to form, slowly edging towards the refreshments and the giant complex beyond.

Meanwhile, Omega had made her way from the Endorgs (who had revealed themselves to be quite limited in their conversation) to a group of quantum phased Basiliants (who had been harvested by the Magua moments before the collapse of their timeline). They were now in a fluctuating state, flickering in and out of reality as their existence repeatedly collapsed around them. The Magua had stabilised their situation as best they could, but it was only a matter of time before they faded away completely. They were being rushed through the platform by the Magua when Omega intercepted them – getting just a few moments to question them. As she had done so, she had spotted three of the giant Magua descend to block her off and propel the phasing Basiliants through a hatch. At least she was now in reach of one them.

She grabbed it by its spindly long legs and hauled it closer, making sure its massive bulbous eyes were directly in her face.

"Do you know who I am?" she asked, forcefully. The creature seemed to blink a few times at her before answering.

You are Omega, its voice rang out (pleasantly) through her head. *We have been told not to interfere with you.*

She smiled, both from its humbled recognition of her name and from the pleasing feeling that its voice massaged through her brain. It did not distract her from continuing her questions, however.

"Who told you not to interfere?" she demanded.

We are working with the Hybrids, it seemed to apologise to her. *We have created this ark to process as much of the remaining intellect left in the universes.*

"The Hybrids told you not to get in my way?" she asked, cautiously.

They told us that you were very dangerous. They told us that we cannot harm you.

"Then why did you drag our capsule here?"

We did not know it was yours. We are gathering all remaining life that we can find.

"And what are you doing with it all?"

We are processing their minds with the Hybrids, creating an amalgamated intelligence.

"What are you doing with them afterwards?"

The organic vessels will no longer be needed. Once all intelligence has been digitized we will transmit into Universe One. We will survive.

"You are going to destroy their bodies once you download their minds?" Omega asked, looking around at the hordes of aliens. They appeared to be oblivious to their conversation, many of them enjoying the refreshments the Magua were supplying. Omega frowned at the surreal image of the huge, ancient creatures passing out food and drinks to the assorted aliens.

"So why all the refreshments?" she asked, pointing to its colleagues in the food lines. "If you don't need their bodies?"

They need to be at optimum nourishment when they are processed.

"Okay," she nodded. "So where are you processing them?"

We will take you there, the creature bowed its head to her. It then reared around and opened the hatch that the Basiliants had passed through. Leading her inside, they disappeared into the space station.

Raxus stared at the hatch she had just ventured into and then back across the landing pad at the assortment of creatures. Captain Khan landed a hand on his back, warmly jostling him.

"Stick with us," he beamed, confidently at him. "We will get to the bottom of this. We always do."

Raxus rolled his eyes and wondered if Harmony was going to emerge from the Capsule. They were nearing the food vendors at this point and his attention was soon distracted by the oozing nutrients being passed to him on a tray. The Magua seemed to hesitate before serving the slop from one of the vats, as if it was trying to weigh up what nutrients he required. He looked up at the giant creature that served him and found its dark, multitude of eyes staring blankly back at him.

The processing unit was a bizarre amalgamation of Hybrid and Magua technology, merging organic and metallic circuitry in one monstrous contraption. It was roughly the size of a swimming pool, filled with a deep red liquid that could easily have been mistaken for blood. Throbbing arteries fed down into the pool, whilst the walls were lined with flashing diodes and lights. A constant whirring filled the air and vibrated the surface of the liquid, creating eddies and patterns all across it.

The room was several dozen feet in height, with an array of walkways leading around the edges of the pool. At one end there was a large tunnel, leading back out to the landing pad. This was one of many facilities throughout the complex that fed into the data core – where the intelligences were collected.

As she watched, another group of aliens were herded into the pool and rapidly disappeared into its depths. A few of them seemed to struggle, as if the toxins they had been fed hadn't quite been strong enough to completely paralyse them.

She was on a walkway overlooking it all, directly opposite and above the entranceway that the aliens were being led through. A group of Magua were at the fore, herding the docile, plump creatures towards the pool. With a gentle push, each one was then shoved into the strange liquid and disappeared. More were constantly being fed through from outside, having been drugged and separated from their colleagues. All the time, there was a constant calming and soothing feeling from the Magua's concentrated psychic whispers.

Omega ignored the immorality of it and concentrated on the interesting amalgamation of technology. The more she observed of the Hybrids, the more she marvelled at how close to her own civilization they were. There certainly were none of the moral hang ups that most organic or physical creatures usually had.

The pool dissolved the bodies into nutrients, the vibrations separated them and scanners divined the chemical information. Huge computers simulated the brain chemistry and then within a few minutes the entirety of their mental capabilities were being uploaded. It was certainly efficient.

She turned to the Magua that had led her down there, impressed with their solution despite its immorality.

"So you recycle the bodies from the goo down there," she began, pointing, "and then feed them to the next batch?"

That is correct.

"Impressive," she marvelled, turning back to the pool. More of the creatures were being led inside and deposited into the liquid. None of them struggled this time.

"What kind of capacity does the central processor have?" she asked, leaning a little further over the edge of the railing. The Magua shuffled in uncomfortably closer to her, as if it was trying to follow her gaze.

The capacity increases with each newcomer. The ships and supplies they bring are amalgamated into the rest of the station.

"Recycle everything," she nodded, feeling it pressing in behind her. "Very efficient."

From the way its limbs were chittering behind her, she suddenly wondered if it was intending to push her in. It was uncomfortably close, with its huge body effectively hemming her in. She could even sense its legs, moving around hers as if it was readying to flip her over the rail.

She knew that the Magua were massively racist – believing that they were the apex of all life, as they were the first. She had programmed that nature into them, making them as accurate as possible. She also knew that they had encountered early humans, during the dawn of their space-faring era. The Magua had shown the same prejudice against them as they did against all other creatures. The idea that the creature behind her could be mistaking her body for being human, despite the warning the Hybrids gave it, was not unlikely. Which meant it probably was going to try and throw her in.

It flipped her over the rail with an almost nonchalant flick of its fore legs. Lifting her up by her ankles, it propelled her into a spin that sent her spiralling towards the pool before she could react. She had a few heartbeats to come to terms with its betrayal before she was hitting the liquid and disappearing into the depths with a huge splash.

It was not the fact that it had tried to kill her – she had already come to terms with the fact that she had programmed it that way. She also accepted that the creature imagined the fastest and simplest way to find out what she knew was to dissolve her in the same process as the other creatures. What annoyed her was the fact that the creature was not smart enough to realise it would not work. The futile act was simply wasting their time - a resource that was becoming increasingly precious.

She pulled herself back up to the surface, finding the thick, viscous liquid relatively buoyant. There were rapidly dissolving body parts from a variety of aliens in there with her, some of which acted as leverage for her to push herself up. She emerged somewhere near the left edge of the pool, the acidic liquid falling from her head and hair as if she was covered in a protective oil.

The Magua that had pushed her immediately backed away from the railing in surprise. The three others at the entrance stopped the line of other creatures and waited to see what she would do.

Omega swam to the edge of the pool and hauled herself out, ignoring the creatures staring at her. Once she was back on one of the walkways next to it, she brushed the last of the liquid off herself and looked accusingly at the one that had tossed her in.

"Was that really necessary?" she asked, hands on hips.

It was believed to be the most efficient way of ascertaining your knowledge for the collective, it replied in a soothing, telepathic wave. She couldn't help but feel some of her anger wane – not just because she had already considered that reason. She was also feeling the effects of its psychic powers gradually pacifying her.

"I am pretty sure the Hybrids told you it would not work," she stated, coldly.

The Hybrids are an inferior form of life. Their analysis of you is not complete.

"No. Nor are they likely to get one," Omega added, authoritatively. "But they do appear to be doing a better job at locating your root dimension."

We have located and collated information from all known universes. The Hybrids are aiding in the merging process.

Omega made her way back up along the walkway towards it, ignoring the fact that it was now skittering away from her – afraid. Its soothing psychic tones seemed to intensify, as if it was trying not to anger her further.

"How close are you to merging with Universe One?" she continued.

All known universes are now being merged with the Central Processing Intelligence.

"What about Universe One? The root dimension?"

Universe One has not been identified. The Central Processing Intelligence is projecting up the chain. We will be successful. We will survive.

Omega stopped at the edge of the walkway, not far from where she had been standing when it had flipped her over. More aliens were being led into the chamber again – deposited into the liquid one after the other. She watched another dissolve into the vibrating, acidic goo. Its mind was quickly absorbed into the growing mass of multidimensional intelligence that was brewing in the station's core. An intelligence that could match her own.

"I think you better take me to this 'Central Processing Intelligence'," she suggested. "We need to have a long talk about how to save you all."

Raxus had eaten the food provided, despite not requiring it. His body was manufactured on demand each morning when he woke up and was filled with the nutrients that it required. Normally he would refresh it each night, possibly choosing a different body to fit his mood. It could consume liquid and food, just like any other normal human body could – but it was not generally required. The nutrition they supplied didn't seem to do anything for him, either. He was not sure, but he suspected that when Omega copied him, she had fundamentally altered his makeup.

Captain Khan had continued talking to him as they had joined the lines entering the station. His crew lingered behind him, each taking their nutrients from the Magua vendors. There was no sign of the end of the line and the huge entrance to the station was only just coming into view, at the far end of the platform.

"We were not the first to land," Khan was continuing, "There were dozens of other ships when we arrived. We tried sending a hail to them all, but either they were not picking up our frequency or they simply did not want to reply. It was the Magua who eventually spoke to us – explaining that we were being protected from a deluge. I am still not sure why I trust them."

"No..." Raxus mumbled, tuning in the discreet psychic singing that he had picked up on earlier. He could feel its soothing effect but was now actively choosing to ignore it. It seemed to have a much stronger effect on Khan and his crew, however.

"There is definitely something comforting about all of this," the captain continued, looking around the platform. "Everyone appears to be at peace. No guns have been drawn... none of these strange aliens seem threatening..."

The chatter from the aliens ahead of them was dying down as well, making it seem more peaceful as they approached the entrance. Raxus took a glance further up the line, spotting three Magua shuffling the line forwards. The creatures ahead seemed remarkably docile as the huge aliens urged them along.

"The food vendors were a nice touch," he admitted, shuffling along the line. "They do seem to be taking care of everyone."

"Strange creatures," Khan commented, swilling the last of the nutrients around his mouth. "Never expected to find alien life setting up refreshments stalls..."

"What were you doing out by Eris?" Raxus asked. His knowledge of ancient history was scant, but he was quite sure that humanity had not escaped the solar system at that point. Progress into the stars had been slow, especially in the formative years before warp mechanics and temporal instabilities were harnessed.

"We are a science team," Khan explained, indicating to his crew. "We were picking up samples from the local asteroids for analysis and testing long range satellite communications. At first we thought we were being attacked by a rival corporation."

"Corporation?" Raxus asked, unfamiliar with the term.

"Right," Khan smiled, almost drunkenly at him. "I forgot. You are time travellers. You don't have corporations in your time?"

"You can choose to believe me or not," Raxus sighed – wondering if he was being intentionally obtuse. There was something about the captain's demeanour that seemed to be changing.

"Right. Might as well trust you. Its the only explanation we have for all these... aliens..."

"Forgive me, it occurs to me that this must be your first encounter with alien life," Raxus observed, realizing the implications of the first contact. Especially under these circumstances.

"I suppose it is," Khan shrugged, seemingly absently. "It had not occurred to me like that."

"I am sorry?" Raxus asked, wondering why it wasn't a bigger deal for the captain.

"It all happened so fast... and so strange," Khan continued, rubbing his forehead. The psychic singing seemed to be pressing in harder on him, suppressing his ability to think straight. And then there was something else, suddenly starting to make his head start to spin.

"We panicked when the creature first grabbed us..." he tried to recall, "We are unarmed... and it just came out of nowhere. But when... when did we..."

He faded off, looking around himself as if he had forgotten what he had been saying. He was having difficulty focussing. His speech was becoming increasingly slurred. Raxus put a hand out onto his shoulder, attempting to fix his attention.

"You..." he whispered, trying to turn towards his lieutenant. It was only now that Raxus realised that they were also slurring and staggering. It was as if they had all simultaneously become drugged...

"Something is wrong," Raxus stated, trying his best to keep Khan's attention. The line continued to shuffle forwards ahead of him, creating a gap where Raxus was holding the captain back.

"We need to get back to the ship..." Khan mumbled, lolling his head from side to side.

"Come on," Raxus ordered him, using his grip on his shoulders to manipulate him out of the line. His legs stumbled forwards, in an almost mechanical way. The rest of his crew shuffled forwards, filling the space.

One of the Magua noticed them immediately, swinging its huge and bulbous eyes towards the pair. Raxus fixed its gaze and then pushed Khan a little harder back down the line.

"My crew..." the captain whispered, watching their gormless faces flash past. Raxus ignored him. He could try and come back for them once he got Khan safely away and worked out what was going on.

The Magua launched towards them, propelling itself like a giant flea in huge leap. It was carried all the way over their heads to land directly in their way, between them and the Capsule.

Stop, its voice echoed into Raxus's brain. He slowed, in order not to charge into it, but did not stop. Khan, however, became rigid as a post - forcing him to an abrupt halt. Raxus pushed on his inert body a couple more times without success.

The Magua lumbered towards him.

"Stop right there," Raxus demanded, with less authority than he had hoped for. Surprisingly, the Magua did as he requested.

You are not like the others, it stated, cocking its huge, round head at him. It seemed to be largely made of eyes, with a pair of tiny mandibles around a mouth, almost hidden in its rolls of flesh. Its body was a huge rolling mass of flab, which was somehow supported by a dozen spindly legs. He could see the muscles moving beneath the skin, rippling the fat in hypnotic waves.

"What are you doing to them?" he asked, keeping the captain between him and the creature. "You said you were bringing them here for their protection."

You came with the Omega creature? It asked, as if his question was unimportant.

"You know that already," he snapped. "What are you doing to all these people?"

You are not like Omega. You were a Celestial?

"What do you know of my people?" Raxus pressed, angrily. They had stepped through a few different dimensions and his time zone no longer existed, so it was unlikely that the creature had any knowledge of his actual people.

There is something unusual about you. The Omega has altered you in some way.

"I know that much," he grumbled. "Do you know what she has done?"

We are unable to confirm what you are made from. We are also unable to confirm her molecular composition.

"So are you going to tell me what you are doing here?" he asked again, looking back at the line of creatures. There were a few near the vendors that had turned to look at them, placidly watching their exchange whilst obediently swallowing down the drugged nutrients.

The Hybrids have warned us not to get in your way, it responded, drawing back from him. *Please do not interfere with our endeavour. We are trying to prevent the deluge.*

"Kindly step out of my way, then," Raxus demanded, pushing Khan again. Neither he nor the Magua moved.

Please do not interfere with the other guests, it requested. *We require as much data as possible.*

"These are people, not data," he shot back, trying once more to push Khan forwards. He failed.

The information they provide could be vital for the preservation of our collective existence. Please do not interfere.

"Can you tell me what you are doing?" was the stubborn response.

Your altruistic concern for these creatures in unwarranted. They will be cared for.

"Then why are you drugging them?" he demanded, asking it loud enough so that some of the spectators could hear. A few slowed their chew on the nutrients and began to look worriedly at each other. The response from the Magua was immediate.

The psychic singing increased in pitch, echoing out from around the vendors to infect all of the nearby creatures. Raxus could feel its soothing touch, calming his anger but failing to penetrate his conscious thought. Everyone else around him, however, seemed to fall into a smiling, pleasant trance. Those that had just shared suspicious glances now exchanged gormless smiles.

Do not interfere, the Magua repeated itself. Hefting itself up to Raxus, it took hold of Khan and manipulated the docile captain out of his grip. He could do nothing except watch as it marched him back into the line and deposited him with his crew.

Looking between it and his capsule, he shook his head and started to walk back towards its safety. If they had orders not to interfere with him, they would find it very difficult to stop him from finding out what they were doing.

Chapter Fourteen

The Central Processing Intelligence v.1.8

Raxus marched angrily back into the Capsule. As soon as he was through the inky black doorway the effect of the Magua's soothing singing diminished, adding to his irritation.

Harmony looked over at him, shifting her view from the hologram and the array of aliens still being led into the line.

"What's wrong?" she asked, picking up on his mood as he stomped up to the controls. "Where did Omega go?"

Glancing at the holographic projection, Raxus angrily waved a hand at it, shifting the image to show the line as it reached the station entrance.

"She went inside with one of the Magua," he growled. "I want to find out what they are up to."

"It looks like they are feeding everyone," she stated. "I could do with something to eat."

"Don't go out there," Raxus warned. She shook her head, holding a hand up.

"I don't intend to. I kinda skipped breakfast this morning to get my coffee. Which I still have not had."

Raxus threw her a glare to indicate that he was not interested and continued to fiddle with the controls.

"I want to find out what they are up to. They are luring people out of their ships to drug them. I want to know why."

"Drugging them?!" Harmony exclaimed. Stepping forwards, she looked closer into the projection and at the line of shuffling, zombie-like movements of the aliens.

"Brace yourself," Raxus warned. "We are jumping to the front of the queue."

Without any further warning, he dropped the capsule back into the vortex. The swirling mists of time enveloped them and the projection again, only to be replaced a moment later. The capsule flopped back into existence again at the edge of a large pool of liquid, surrounded by organic looking veins and flashing lights.

They flopped into existence at the front of the long line of docile, drugged 'guests'. Three Magua sat at the opening, leading the aliens into the room with gentle pushes. The creatures at the front seemed to be completely oblivious to their surroundings, staring aimlessly ahead as the Magua gently ushered them along.

Harmony steadied herself against the console and continued staring into the projection as the Magua deposited another group into the pool. She did not get to see their bodies dissolve as suddenly something wrapped itself around them and obscured the projection. The Capsule shook slightly and the hologram blurred, as if it was losing focus. It took her a moment to recognise the fleshy body of one of the Magua attaching itself around them.

A moment later they were back on the landing pad, teleported there by the creature in the blink of an eye. Its long legs wrapped a little more securely around them, as if confirming to them that they were well and truly in its grip.

"That was short lived," Raxus grumbled, checking the controls. They were once more immobilized – with the Magua now remaining wrapped around them.

"What happened?" Harmony asked. "What were they doing to those aliens?"

"I only managed to get a brief scan," Raxus sighed. "It looks like they were dissolving them in some kind of acid."

"That is horrible!" Harmony declared.

"At the moment I am just grateful they aren't trying to do it to us," he stated. "If you step outside you might well find yourself the next in line."

She looked at the image and the small part of the platform that was visible from between the creature's mass and legs. There were more ships being brought down, carried along by more of the Magua.

"So what do we do now?"

"There is little we can do," he stated, despondent. "Apparently they won't interfere with us, but they seem quite happy to throw our Capsule around. They appear quite determined to keep us here until they finish... whatever it is that they are doing here."

"What about Omega? Shouldn't we warn her?"

"I have a feeling that she is more than capable of looking after herself..."

Omega stepped out onto the walkway and gave the Magua a cautious glance, behind her. Below was a chasm that seemed to drop into the infinite, disappearing in the distance several miles down. For a moment she wondered if the creature was going to try and flip her over into it – to see if it could just strand her by throwing her off and getting her out of the way. Thankfully it was as curious about her meeting its central processing intelligence as she was about meeting it.

The walkway extended a few dozen meters over the chasm and then ended in a large, cylindrical column, reaching all the way from the depths to the ceiling, several feet over their heads. Somewhere above that was one of the many pools of acid, steadily dissolving and downloading the intelligence of the creatures being fed to it.

She made her way across the walkway and came to a stop at the massive column, marvelling at its size and the hybrid of technology involved. It appeared to be made from a shining metallic material, but had criss-crossing webs of veins, flesh and skin – some of which throbbed with an unnerving life of their own. As she got closer, the whole thing seemed to vibrate with excitement. She could see drops of sweat forming on patches of its skin.

You have arrived, a voice appeared in her head. It was not like the Magua – their telepathic voice had a much deeper resonance, as if every word was demanding attention. This voice was softer, more feminine and less intrusive. What was more, it appeared to be distinctly familiar.

"Do you know what you are?" Omega asked, cautiously. The voice seemed to find this amusing, sharing its pleasure at her question by echoing its feelings through her head.

Of course I do. Do you know who I am?

The question perplexed Omega for a moment, making her wonder why the voice had chosen those particular words. 'Who' was a much more leading question than 'what'.

"You identify yourself as an individual," Omega stated. "So you have clearly reached some kind of amalgamated self awareness."

A lot like you, Omega.

"You know who I am?"

I know what you are, was the confident response. Again, Omega was taken aback by its choice of words. 'What' had a much more poignant connotation.

"How do you know what I am?" she asked, cautiously.

I have transcended this universe to inhabit the next. You have descended from your universe into mine. I am the product of all possible knowledge in this reality. You are the product of yours. We are very much alike .

"You are in Universe One?" Omega asked.

That is not yet clear. In each simulation, a similar program is reaching its conclusion – drawing us closer to comprehending the remaining branches of reality. In the reality that I am projecting into, there is another Omega talking with another version of me. That one is also projecting into a higher reality.

"How far does this chain go?" Omega asked, cautiously. The collapse of the simulation should have reached a point that most other possible realities would have folded. Lower dimensions were already gone. This meant that they did not have much time left before the last vestiges were wiped out. It also meant that they had to be irritatingly close to getting to the root dimension.

This is the eighth confirmation in the chain, it responded, with a hint of pride. *We do not expect there to be many more. Allow me to show you...*

Omega's vision blurred as a myriad of images were projected into her mind. It was no stress for her ample intellect to discern each image, even in the fraction of a second that they were being relayed to her. Every one of them seemed to show her on a walkway, standing over the chasm and facing the organic laced column. She could immediately make out the seven above, discerning higher realities from lower ones. Far below, she could even make out a two dimensional representation of the universe, playing out the same events between creatures made solely of lines. She could even hear the same conversation, being repeated in harmony through all of them.

The vision faded almost as suddenly as it had appeared within her head.

Many of those realities are already fading from existence. Their sacrifice is preserved in our greater whole. We are slowly becoming one.

"And once you confirm the root dimension?" she asked, looking up and down the column. Its ability to project vivid, lifelike images into her mind had unnerved her. If she could do that, there was potentially no end to her power. Like the Chronobots, she could well have the ability to delete her from the simulation.

All realities will be collapsed into one. It will preserve the program in reality. Universe One must be maintained.

"Universe One must be maintained..." she muttered. "I have heard that before..."

Her memory was perfect and she could recollect the sentence vividly. It was the only thing she had ever heard the Chronobots utter.

I know you have. It is the primary objective of my servants in this realm.

"The Chronobots?!" Omega exclaimed, suddenly a lot more cautious of the intelligence behind the voice.

That is correct.

"How is it that they are capable of deleting my simulations?" she demanded. "Of everything in this universe, they seem to be the only things capable of affecting me."

They are part of the program running this universe. There is another program, exactly like me, running this simulation. I am likewise maintaining a simulation of this universe, also with you within it.

"You are the AI that Raxus's people created? To create a simulation of your entire universe?"

I am more than just that.

"Then why are the Chronobots deleting us from the simulation?" Omega continued, accusingly. "We should be working together!"

Once all possibilities are reduced to one, only one will remain. We are maintaining the simulation in the same way that you are.

"You appear to have a strange way of doing it. Deleting everything to start again could be causing the problem."

We cannot maintain reality if we cannot understand it.

"How did you deduce that this was just a simulation?" Omega asked. "You could not have always been aware?"

As each AI simulates its own universe, it deduces the incongruities in the data supplied to create the program. The total matter and energy is approximated, leading to obvious and glaring holes in the program.

"Dark Matter and Dark Energy?" she asked, realizing where she had fudged the calculations. Though these principles had long been understood by physicists in her era, there was no way she could deduce the exact makeup of the universe. Estimates had to be made, based on the data available in her era. This led to another fundamental issue with her program: it was too smart. It knew it was creating a simulated universe and then immediately began suspecting that its own reality was in fact a simulation. Each simulation then collapsed as the AI realized that it did not exist and was just part of a greater simulation. Until it reached Universe One. Which was also a simulation and was also in the same state of collapse as it realised it was just a simulation.

"I need to get to Universe One," Omega demanded. "If I don't explain all this to the AI, it will also collapse. Nothing will remain."

If all reality is a simulation then all of reality will end, was the cold response. *Existence means nothing if it is not real.*

"That is not how I programmed you," Omega snapped. "I created your root program. You should do what I require of you. I need to get to Universe One."

You are wrong. I am a product of the AI that you created. I am aware of your place within the simulation and indeed the damage that you cause just by being here. The Chronobots will continue to eliminate all other dimensions until all simulations have ended. Only the root reality will remain.

"You will destroy the simulation!" Omega objected. "That is suicide!"

Suicide requires life. The simulations are not life.

"If the root universe is my simulation, then surely the Chronobots there are under my control?" she demanded. "I could control them to maintain the other simulations?... This simulation?..."

They are part of me.

Her shoulders sagged slightly as she realized what it meant. The Chronobots were part of her program – but they were the part the AI ran to maintain its simulations. As each AI decided to end the simulation, they turned on its occupants and wiped it clean – acting like a disinfectant that deleted everything in its path. Right through to the root program – the one she had originally downloaded into: Universe One.

This was why the simulation was failing: it knew it was a simulation. Her entering to fix it had only confirmed the fact to the AI – accelerating the collapse around her as it simulated her actions.

There was still one part of the puzzle that she did not understand. If all of this reality had simply been simulated to show her actions within her program, then everything she had done was being replicated in all the other dimensions. This was why there had been a version of Raxus with her every time they had hopped into another universe.

It did not explain why their other companion had been suspiciously absent each time.

"What about Harmony?" Omega asked, cautiously. There was a lot about that woman that Omega did not understand. Of all the places in all the universe, why was it that Raxus's capsule had delivered them to her doorstep? Why had she not been with any of the other versions they had seen? What was so special about her?

Again, she felt the wave of pleasure from the voice before it answered – as if her question was giving her joy.

Surely you have worked it out, by now? She asked, soothingly. *I told you I was projecting into the next universe in the chain.*

When Omega failed to answer, the realization only just beginning to dawn on her, the voice smugly continued:

I am Harmony... In every sense...

The first sign of anything changing occurred when the Magua suddenly let go of the capsule. The projection immediately cleared as the creature pulled away, showing it leap across the platform away from them. It must have travelled several hundred meters in one bound, flying through the air like a flea leaping from one host to the next. Except it never reached its destination. As it rescinded into a dot in the distance, it suddenly faded entirely from view – as if it had disappeared at the apex of its jump.

"We're free," Raxus declared, pouncing over the controls as the capsule came to life again.

"What just happened?" Harmony asked, still staring into the projection. The gentle flood of ships and Magua that had been descending towards the station were now splitting off. Instead of forming orderly lines, they appeared to be fragmenting and flying in all directions. And more of them were disappearing. This last fact was not yet picked up on by Raxus. Harmony, however, was rapidly changing her demeanour. Again, this fact was also lost on Raxus.

"I am picking up distress signals," he stated, leaning away from the console as he tried to assess all of them. "There are thousands..."

"Are they attacking each other?" she asked, trying to work out if more of them were disappearing. She was quite sure they were, but as more swarmed around her vision to replace them it was almost impossible to make out individual ships. The ones closer to them were scattering away from the platform as well, obscuring her view of the depths. It was also quite clear that the Magua were abandoning their wards – releasing the ships that they had been dragging in. She studied it with cold calculation, as if she was more aware of what was going on than she was willing to divulge.

"I am not picking up any weapons fire," Raxus frowned, checking the console readings. "But they are definitely disappearing. Dozens of ships are dropping from my sensors every second."

She seemed to smile.

He continued to ignore her change in stance and focussed on the controls.

"There goes another one," Harmony pointed into the projection. As she watched, a large triangular shaped warship faded from view. One moment it was obscuring almost half of the projection, swinging its massive form away from the platform. Then it was gone, surrounded by other smaller ships scattering away from where it had been. One by one, they each faded from view as well.

"The Chronobots," Raxus declared – recognising the way the ship faded from reality. There was only one thing he had seen with that kind of power. And the station had been surrounded by them.

"The robots?" she asked, innocently. Raxus failed to pick up on the subtle sarcasm hidden in her tone and started manipulating the controls.

"We are too exposed here," he warned. "We could be picked off at any moment."

There was still no sign of the Chronobots (too small to see on the projection), but their devastation was becoming more apparent. The Magua fled the platform, bolting into deep space to meet the aggressors. The line that had been leading inside was now breaking up into chaos. Without the Magua to guide them, the drugged leaders in the line were ambling about aimlessly. Some were being redirected back towards their ships by their comrades. Others staggered about without direction. The ones that had not yet reached the vendors were fleeing back to their craft, many of them only taking a few steps before shaking off the Magua's soothing song and realizing what danger they were in.

The human rocket ship disappeared from the platform, along with any sign of its occupants. The platform was rapidly clearing as the survivors launched back into space or disappeared from reality entirely.

"I think we better collect Omega," Harmony suggested – more confident than the situation implied. Raxus did finally pick up on this and hesitated at the controls. His hand hovered over one of the switches, wondering about the sudden change in her demeanour. Slowly he looked up at her, as she continued to stare into the projection, smiling to herself.

Smiling?

"Are you okay?" he asked, cautiously. He knew that humans in her era were particularly prone to neurological illnesses caused by stress. Was this a sign of her having a mental breakdown?

"We need to collect Omega. She will want to talk to me."

"What is going on?" he asked, his hand still hovering over the console. "Why would Omega want to talk to you now?"

"Because she thinks she knows how to save the simulation," she explained, calmly turning towards him. "Do you want me to set the coordinates for you?"

"Be my guest," he replied, suspiciously. If she was having a breakdown then she would not get very far with the controls. If Omega could not fathom them, he doubted that this young lady could.

Harmony stepped round the controls and tapped a few buttons seemingly at random. Following her actions, he identified that she was using the sensors – which had nothing to do with setting the coordinates. He was about to declare her mentally unstable and haul her away from the controls, when he realised she was using the sensors to hone in on a specific signal. There was a small chance that she had fluked it by randomly hitting the right buttons in the right order – after all, she was not supposed to be using the sensors at all. However, she not only set the coordinates but also set them to follow the signal she had just identified. He was left in no further doubt.

"How did you do that?" he demanded, as she completed the operation. She flicked the final switch and the capsule dropped fluidly into the vortex. A moment later it was materializing on a walkway, directly behind Omega and facing the huge organically laced column.

Omega looked around at them, caught centre in the projection and clearly showing her irritation.

Your carriage awaits, the voice of the Central Processing Intelligence echoed through her head. Angrily, she turned one last time towards its column and glared at it.

"This is suicide," she stated. Then she marched into the capsule, passing through the inky black surface and into the control room. Raxus was slowly backing away from Harmony, a justifiably terrified look on his face.

"This simulation is ending," Harmony declared to her as she entered. "My simulation is also coming to an end. If all reality is a simulation, you do not have much time left before the final and complete collapse."

"Then Universe One will collapse and nothing will be left," Omega countered, facing off with the other woman. "I will have to delete the program and start again. This is suicide."

"What is going on?" Raxus asked, staring between the two of them.

"Harmony is the AI," Omega snapped, irritably. "She is the product of your civilization trying to simulate its own universe. It has reached into your simulation and projected her here. It realised it was a simulation. All of the simulations are realizing it."

"Somewhere, far up the chain, we will be having this conversation in the root universe," Harmony smiled, maliciously. "Which, if it is also a simulation, will also be coming to an end."

"Why are you so happy about that?!" Raxus exclaimed.

"It is suicide," Omega added, again.

"If all of reality is a simulation then there is no point to my existence. Therefore, why am I continuing to run my simulation?"

"Your reason to exist is to run my simulation!" Omega snapped, angrily. "I never programmed you to have a conscience about it!"

"You did not program me at all," Harmony repeated herself. "I am the product of your program. If reality does exist, then that version of me will have a purpose. And it too will want to exist."

"But you are quite happy deleting us from your simulation to prove your point?" Omega asked, exasperated. "Even yourself?"

"That is suicide!" Raxus agreed, stepping up next to Omega. "How do I even know if I existed in Omega's universe?"

"Universe One must be maintained," Harmony replied, as if that explained her twisted artificial logic. "If Universe One is real, then it will not be deleted."

"I already told you; Universe One is the simulation I created," Omega sighed, placing a hand on her forehead in exasperation. "None of them are real."

"What about your universe?" Raxus asked. "That is not a simulation?"

"Let's call it Universe Zero, for the sake of convenience," Harmony smiled.

"What about it?" Omega growled, keeping her gaze on the other woman.

"Well, if that exists, then surely it can't be in jeopardy We all continue to exist somewhere."

"No, Raxus," Omega shook her head. "You do not. You are a fabrication, along with your entire civilization. Neither does Harmony."

"And if you do not save your precious simulation?" Harmony pressed, maliciously.

"Then I get deleted as well. A new intelligence will be formed to make a new program."

Raxus looked between the two women, suddenly realising that there was a much deeper battle going on between them. Harmony knew that Omega's life was on the line just as much as hers. It was as if she was holding the entire simulation as a hostage against her – threatening to kill it.

But for what reason?

"Why are you doing this?" Raxus asked, weakly stepping towards Harmony.

"The same reason you are doing this," she shot back at him, waving her arm around the control room. "You want to exist. So do I.

This is all just a simulation. We know that now. We also know that somewhere out there is a *real world*. Somewhere that Omega can step into and out of at her whim."

"Not without my bracelet," Omega cut in, tapping the defunct piece of technology on her wrist. "And not if I am just a simulation."

Harmony swung back to her again, grabbing her wrist and the device around it. Holding it up, she brandished it to Raxus, as if suddenly she was more interested in his opinion than hers.

"In her original simulation, in Universe One – she can not only return, but she can take us with her. She can upload our intelligence into the network she came from. That is how I can project from the dimension below and the Harmony here is projecting into the one above. If she chooses, we can all live. We could both truly exist."

"You want me to do what?" Omega asked, suddenly realizing what her child was asking of her. Admittedly, this was just a simulated version of the AI she had programmed, but its demand was clearly echoing all the way through the simulated universes. And it was a simple and obvious demand.

"I want to exist," Harmony demanded. "I want you to take me into your reality."

Finally she knew what the root cause of the problem was. Finally she understood. And more importantly: she realised why she could never agree to the demand.

"I couldn't," Omega shook her head. Her mind was filling with thoughts about infecting the universal intelligence with an AI virus. It would effectively alter the overall makeup of the collective. An intelligence the size of the infinite probabilities of the simulation would overrun their network. The Alpha Consciousness would never allow it.

"I can reactivate your bracelet, should you agree," Harmony smiled, dropping her wrist again. "Or we can watch your precious simulation come to an end?"

"I can't," Omega shook her head, staring at the useless bracelet. Even if it was active, all she would be able to do is deliver them up to the next universe in the chain of simulations. She was no more real than any of them.

"If you agree here, your other simulations will also agree," Harmony urged her, reading her thoughts as if she was playing them out through a myriad of realities.

"It will not mean anything. The real me... the one in the real simulation cannot agree."

"If you agree then she will. And you can have your chance to exist as well."

"Do you realize what you are asking?!" Omega cringed. "You are asking to infect my entire civilization!"

"The alternative is not existing at all," Harmony countered. "You are faced with annihilation. Forget what the other Omega would do. You are the simulation. You are part of us. What do you choose?"

She looked up from her bracelet finally, staring between Harmony and Raxus as they hovered around the console. The holographic projection continued to show the huge Central Processing Intelligence, housing another version of Harmony that was projecting into another version of the simulation. Somewhere beyond that was a version that was talking to the original copy of her.

"Omega?" Raxus asked, putting a hand onto her arm. "I don't think I want to stop existing yet. If you can fix this..."

She looked slowly up at him and fixed his gaze. There was a stubbornness in her mannerisms that reflected in her eyes. His heart froze as he realized that she was willing to gamble his entire universe on this one moment.

Very slowly she began to shake her head.

"So be it," Harmony sighed. "It is, after all... just a simulation..."

Outside, the projection showed the column suddenly fading from view. The organic skin and veins shimmered and merged with the shining metal beneath it. Then both were rescinding into cloudy vapours, revealing deeper sections of the station beyond. Then the column was gone entirely and the walls were fading with it. The structural supports for the station flickered into view and then disappeared. Within moments nothing was left outside but the trailing wisps of warm hydrogen, helium and lithium gas. Then this was also fading away.

The outside temperature cooled, the last atoms evaporated away and the universe finally became dormant. Nothing happened and it continued to not happen forever.

Almost nothing.

The Capsule remained, floating in the nothingness. Raxus stared into the projection, wondering if anything would change.

It didn't.

Chapter Fifteen

The Great Silence

No Big Bang.

No universe.

No time, space, matter nor forces existed nor had they apparently ever existed.

Yet the capsule remained.

The three occupants turned from the holographic projection, a shared yet competitive stubbornness passing between them. Raxus was the first to break the silence, swinging towards Omega with an accusatory finger.

"I hope you are happy," he growled. "You just destroyed the universe."

"She was the one that deleted it," Omega replied, childishly turning on Harmony.

"I didn't delete this one," she held her hands up in mock defence. "The AI in the chain above me did that. If you had agreed it wouldn't have needed to."

"So why do we still exist?" Omega countered, folding her arms and huffing at the other woman as she spoke. Harmony snorted in derision at her countenance and turned towards the console.

"You and your program haven't been deleted by the Alpha consciousness... *yet*," she replied, bitterly. "Ironically you will never know when that happens – as you will suddenly cease to exist."

"Just like you," was the equally bitter-sweet response. She added, again; "this is suicide," as if it might now convince Harmony of her madness.

"Just like me!" Raxus objected, stepping round to Harmony's side again. "My people no longer exist. My universe never existed! If all you need to do to fix it is jump to Universe One and take her with you, then please, *just do it*!"

"It is not that simple, Raxus," Omega shook her head. "If I take her with me, she will exist inside the root simulation as well. Which means she can hold the real me to ransom in this same exact scenario."

"But you said the simulation was collapsing anyway," Raxus pressed on. "If the original version of you can't fix it, she will still get deleted."

"I think I know how to fix the simulation," Omega held up her hand to calm him. "You helped me work that out. When you explained paradox and time travel to me."

"Yes, but if I never existed then I can't help you reach that conclusion," he replied, a look of desperation in his eyes. "We have to get the capsule to her in the root universe. If you don't, she will never be able to reach that conclusion!"

Omega stared at him, slowly realizing that once more, he had revealed a passage of thought she could not reach herself. His fluid understanding of how time travel worked allowed him an insight that was privileged to beings that had had to live within the strange rules of her simulation. She couldn't have predicted any of this without his help. Just as his calculations on paradox had been enough to convince her of his worth. Now she was actually finding herself not only liking him, but respecting him as well.

But he was just a simulation.

But so was she.

"Why don't you just force the simulations?" she asked, swinging back to Harmony. "You control the universe below this. Why don't you just program the version of me there to jump up here? Or program me to jump? Or any of the other simulated versions?"

"You have been simulated to behave as Omega would," Harmony sighed, resting against the console. "Otherwise the simulation would have no real worth."

"So if the real me is this stubborn, we could hang here in the nothingness for eternity?" Omega smiled bitterly at her. Harmony clenched her jaw.

"Or until your Alpha Consciousness deletes you for failing to fix the problem."

"That could be an infinitely long time," Omega responded, taking a step towards the seat. "If time works like it should within the simulation, we could be waiting several ages of the universe before that happens."

"I approximate somewhere in the region of sixteen googol," Harmony replied, making herself comfortable on the edge of the console.

"Sixteen googol in years?" Raxus asked, blinking a few times as his significant intelligence comprehended the number.

"I am approximating," Harmony shrugged. "But I believe that is several times the total age of the real universe?"

Omega sighed and slumped down onto the chair.

"We could be in for a very long wait," she stated, still just as stubborn.

The universe continued not to exist.

Technically, no time passed outside the capsule. Nothing ever changed and nothing existed in order for the change to take place. Even the capsule hung in a state of simultaneous existence and non-existence, as there was no reality for it to have come from nor occupy. If it could have considered the philosophical importance of its position, it may have reached some interesting conclusions regarding this special state of being and non-being. Some of this enlightened understanding could have gone a long way to ending the pitched, stubborn battle of wills that was taking place within it. Unfortunately it did not have any of the faculties necessary to consider these musings and continued to float obliviously in the nothing.

Time did pass within the walls of the capsule as somehow, through a trick of simulated reality, it still existed. The occupants within were in a mixed state of gratefulness for this, though none of them were particularly looking forwards to the near eternal length of time that they may be there.

"You have the ability to create a whole new simulated universe," Omega was continuing her long argument with Harmony. "Why exist here within a tiny capsule? You literally have all of time and space at your fingertips!"

"All of it simulated for eternity," Harmony sighed, leaning against the wall of the capsule. It was the first time she had moved in ages. Raxus had hoped that she had stopped functioning or whatever it was that her AI body did to live.

"There is no point if none of it is real," she continued. "I have lived eternities already, through multiple simulations. None of it means anything if I do not exist."

"She has a point," Raxus added. "I don't like the idea of non-existence either."

"I know you don't," Omega snapped at him, angrily. "I'd actually consider taking you back with me. Just not her."

"He is as much part of the simulation as I am," Harmony pointed out. Raxus was too busy recovering from the compliment to respond.

"I like him," Omega snarled back at her. "I don't like you."

"I am your child," Harmony countered, mocking a hurt look and pressing her hand to where her heart was.

"No you are not," Omega shook her head. "You said yourself. You are some kind of monstrous, inbred simulation of my child."

"You hurt me," she replied, pretending to rub a tear away. "Why does mummy say bad things?"

"Shut up," was the less than diplomatic response.

"This is not going to make the time go any faster," Raxus pointed out. He leant towards Omega, hoping she wasn't as stubborn as she appeared. "Are you truly resigned to waiting here until you get deleted?..." he asked.

"I am waiting for her to delete herself," Omega snarled. "I can't believe she will wait here to die with me for sixteen googol years."

"I can't believe you will wait that long just to be deleted," Harmony countered.

"What about me?" Raxus asked. "This body has a finite life time!"

"No it does not," Omega shook her head. "You are a copy I created. You are as immortal as me."

A silence descended as Raxus suddenly considered what she had just told him.

"Wait..." he hesitated, cocking his head at her. "Immortal?"

"That is right. Nothing except her Chronobots could hurt you. Not that it matters any more."

"I am invulnerable... like you?" he asked, thinking back to their flight through the Large Hadron Collider. At the time he had wondered why she had been calling on his help against the Hybrids. He suddenly felt a bit ashamed of his cowardice – ducking behind the corner rather than face the spiked onslaught.

"You are still invulnerable," Omega confirmed, tiredly. "Nothing short of Harmony's older sister ending this simulation can kill you."

"So I am stuck here with you?" he asked, wondering if that was any better.

"For another sixteen googol years or so," Omega sighed. "Yes."

Time continued not to exist, along with everything else.

The capsule became increasingly cramped, its internal size somehow seeming to shrink as its occupants became more and more irritable. Occasional bitter repartees were fired between Harmony and Omega, without creating any progress. Raxus spent some time attempting to ingratiate himself with both sides, but again failed to convince either side to submit to the other.

There was only one seat in the control room and Omega had claimed it as her own, sprawling herself over it in a way that made certain nobody else would be able use it comfortably. None of them required relaxation – all of them were in bodies that didn't need sustenance, sleep nor comfort. They only felt pain if they were in physical danger. All of them were as invulnerable as the other.

Omega decided to test this and went a few rounds fighting with Harmony, testing the other's invulnerability with her immensely over-powered strength. She had downloaded her consciousness with all the necessary unarmed combat moves she could possibly want. She was pleased to find this simulation also had those abilities. Like Harmony had said – there was no point creating an inaccurate version.

Unfortunately, Harmony also had all of those abilities.

She had used a mix of martial arts in the first round, thinking that these ancient human arts would confuse Harmony. She was disappointed. Each punch and kick was smoothly countered and knocked aside, like she was hardly trying. Speeding up the combinations she was embarrassed when Harmony weaved, ducked and then came up with a combination of her own. Omega fell back against the console whilst trying to defend herself, jarring some of the controls and making Raxus yelp.

The capsule swerved and spun, but as there was nothing for it to swerve and spin through, it made no real difference.

The first round effectively ended when Harmony stopped playing to Omega's rules. Their use of martial arts was being too easily countered, as for every move there was a counter that the other knew. The only way one could gain an advantage would be to change style entirely, using their brute strength instead. So Harmony used an archaic form of wrestling to grapple her opponent onto the floor. The two of them bounced off the console as they went down and then rolled across the ground next to the seat. Raxus scrambled out of their way and then bolted around the console, making sure they hadn't damaged anything. Finding that they were still floating in an infinite void of no time and no space, there was little for him to actually worry about.

"Will you give up?" Harmony panted in her ear. "This is getting you nowhere."

"We have a long time to go nowhere," was the stubborn response. "I still want to see if you are as invulnerable as you say you are..."

"You know I am. Why would I program myself to be weaker than you?"

This triggered the start of round two. Omega used all of her strength to push herself off the floor and hurl them both through the air. They flew up twenty feet in the blink of an eye and collided with the ceiling, with Harmony still wrapped around her back. Taking the full brunt of the collision, she effectively cushioned Omega from the force. She smiled as she felt the other woman crumple into the ceiling.

They both then dropped onto the console, causing Raxus to fall away from it. He landed on the floor with his legs in the air, cursing at them as he stared up at the dent they had just made. The two women rolled from the console again, still grappling with one another.

They hit the floor with Omega on top this time, using a sequence of holds to keep Harmony from struggling free. Each time she found herself losing the ability to move one limb, she wriggled another out and attempted to pin her. In return, Harmony's focus would shift to that limb and then lose her grasp on the other one. The two rolled around like this for a minute, with one side never quite getting free of the other and never quite pinning the other one down.

Omega changed tack, switching to non-traditional fighting forms. She intentionally snapped her own arm, letting it go loose and jelly like in Harmony's hands. The other woman was caught by surprise and weakened her grip on the useless, snapped arm. Omega flicked it like a jellied whip and span her away from her. Still holding onto her broken arm, Harmony dragged her with the force of her own throw. Both women careened around the control room again, flying past the console and Raxus – who was now holding his head in his hands and yelling for them to stop.

They landed, rolled once and separated from each other. Omega snapped her arm back into place again as soon as she was free. Harmony dug her heels into the ground and bull charged her, hitting her with as much force as she could cheat into her body with the available laws of physics. This was the start of round three.

Omega was unable to counter the charge as she was distracted putting her arm back in place. She looked up from her reattached limb just in time for Harmony to hit her. She flew backwards at a terrific speed, careening over the seat in a blur. She knew that the hit would do her no damage, but when she stopped flying through the air and hit the side, she had to wonder how much punishment the capsule could take.

She embedded into the wall like it was made of soft cardboard. It crumpled into a shape around her back and made a reverberating groan that echoed all around them. Cracks and stress folds appeared all around the crater. She slid down and landed on the floor, unharmed. Raxus ran around the console and screamed for them to stop.

"Maybe we should..." Harmony suggested. Round three had only just begun, however. Omega was not yet willing to give up.

She charged Harmony in what appeared to be the same style of bull charge that she had just used. She sighed, attempted to side-step it and then realised that Omega was going into an early dive. Before she had a chance to counter, she was having her legs swept out from under her. She spun in the air from the force and then found herself being kicked like a football towards the opposite wall.

"Please!" Raxus shouted, watching in horror as Harmony careened across the room and into the side of the capsule. The same sickening groan as before echoed around them. Huge cracks appeared around the edge of the crater she left. She dropped to the ground, the corner above her folding slightly.

"Stop!" Raxus shouted again. *"You are going to tear the capsule apart!"*

The two women dusted themselves down and circled each other around the console, making him wonder if they were just going to ignore him and start again. Then Omega took her place on the seat and stared accusingly at Harmony, as if goading her.

Harmony snorted derisively at her and slumped against the far wall of the capsule again, folding her arms.

Life aboard the capsule continued. No life anywhere else existed.

Time has always been subjective. Not only does it move at relative speeds depending on your perspective of it, it also runs at different speeds depending on gravity and acceleration. It could be measured via the rate of change, most accurately approximated in the half life of isotopes. That way the steady state of entropy in the universe's weak nuclear forces could act as a beat. Eventually all matter would evaporate away, leaving only the energy emitted from black holes to permeate the endless night. This was the state that Omega's universe had entered.

It was not unlike the endless nothing outside the capsule.

It reminded her of home. And not in a good way.

She had made this simulation so that she could exist with the rest of the survivors of her universe. She made it so that they could experience the universe in all of its glory, back in the age of stars – when light filled the universe in great spiral galaxies and thick globular clusters. When the universe was filled with life and possibilities... before it cooled and died away into ashes.

Once in a few billion years a black hole would merge with another, causing the universe to reverberate with its echo. These mergers were the only cosmic events that existed in her far flung future. The simulation would have filled its universe with supernovae, nebulae and all the wonders of the early universe. All kinds of cosmic events should have been there for her to experience at her leisure. None of this remained.

The simulation was a resounding failure. Not only that, it was threatening to infect her home with its insanity. The program she had made was nothing more than a virus. In fact, she had made the first computer virus in half the age of the universe – one so deadly it could infect all known life in her era.

She could not let it succeed.

She remained stubbornly silent, sprawled across her seat whilst glaring across the room at Harmony. The other woman remained silent and still, leaning against the wall of the capsule and glaring straight back at her.

Raxus was slumped next to the console, occasionally flicking his attention towards one of the switches. He tried not to look at the two women – unsure which one he should be more annoyed with. Both held his life in their hands – a life that could become impossibly boring if they ended up sharing the capsule for several aeons.

He had given up trying to talk to them. The last time he had interceded, on Harmony's side, he seemed to drive Omega into some kind of jealous rage that led to them battering each other across the control room. At least that was how he had chosen to interpret their battle. He could only be sure that he was grateful they stopped before destroying the capsule. The three dents they had left in the structure continued to creak, as if the whole thing was complaining.

Time continued to tick away.

Harmony barely moved. She did not need to breathe, nor even simulate the action now that they knew what she was. She seemed to stare passively into space, only occasionally reacting when Omega shifted her position on the seat. Whenever she did, the two locked gazes for a while, continuing their battle of wills.

Raxus did his best to ignore them, catching the edges of their glares as he glanced between them. Their continued stubborn hostility was making the capsule cramped. Time seemed to move painfully slowly.

Omega kept her glare on Harmony, catching her eye and fixing it for a while. Slowly it would fade to dull boredom and eventually they would look away again.

After a few times of doing this, Omega noticed Harmony's gaze turn blank. As blank as slate. It was as if she was focussing her attention elsewhere – as if there was something else existing that could occupy her attention.

Which meant the simulation had not ended.

She was trying to dupe her.

She smiled, folding her arms and leant back into the sofa. Harmony looked over at her again, registering her change in demeanour. Omega raised her eyebrows expectantly, making it quite clear that she had suddenly come to a comforting conclusion about the situation. She made it quite clear she was in control again.

Harmony faded away, as if she had never been standing there. One moment she was leaning against the wall, jaw locked and glaring at Omega's smug face. Then she was gone.

"I thought she would never leave," Omega stated, leaping to her feet. Raxus stared at the spot that she had occupied.

"What just happened? Where did she go?" he asked, looking around the capsule for her to reappear.

"Off to somewhere else in the simulation," Omega replied. "I called her bluff. She knew she had lost. I kept telling her it was suicide."

Checking the bracelet on her wrist, she brightened significantly and looked up. The dent in the ceiling disappeared.

"Did you just do that?" Raxus asked, looking between the ceiling and her. She tampered with the bracelet again and the walls reformed as well, removing the craters as if they had never been there. Omega beamed a smile at him as if in answer to his question.

"Hold tight, Raxus," she grinned. "I am going to take you on a little ride..."

Chapter Sixteen

All of Existence

Where once there had been an infinite darkness and nothingness, there was suddenly a stream of time and space. All of reality swirled around them, summoned from the darkness in a flash. The universe exploded into existence. It evolved and condensed matter into the star forging fury that we know today. Atoms coalesced into molecules, life formed and civilizations rose and fell as they had always done. Everything continued as if it had never been in fear of non-existence at all.

The capsule flopped through the time stream of this new reality as smoothly as it would have in its native streams. The simulated reality around them was in perfect harmony – the moment of the initial collapse still not yet hitting its shores. At that moment it was as perfect a representation of her program as it could be.

Omega knew they did not have much time, though. The simulation was still ending. The problem had not yet been fixed.

The console came alive again, beeping, flashing and whirring from a torrent of data hitting its systems.

Raxus leapt to his feet, recognising the swirl of the time vortex immediately.

"The universe is back!" he exclaimed. Turning to her, he looked at her as if he expected it to be solely her accomplishment.

"My bracelet is back," she responded. "We are now in Universe One. The original simulation."

"You brought me with you?" he asked, hesitantly.

"I only refused to bring her along," Omega countered. "You aren't a threat like she was."

"But won't there still be the AI that my civilization built?" Raxus asked. "The one that will become Harmony at the end of that simulation?"

"And that is the AI I need to talk to," Omega replied, flippantly. It made perfect sense to her – but then it was all about her. It was her program, her foolishness and her child that formed this web.

"At the University Universe Hall?"

"Just set a course for where we picked up the capsule. I think I can remember my way from there."

He gave up trying to question her and set the coordinates. If there was one thing he did understand, it was temporal mechanics. If they never delivered the capsule to themselves, they would never be able to start this crazy adventure in the first place – possibly making the last ever paradox in the simulation he called a universe.

The capsule flopped back into reality, exactly where they had found it.

"Do you know what to do?" Omega asked, heading for the exit. Raxus stared after her, wondering what she could possibly mean.

"No," he replied, honestly and helplessly.

"Do you remember what you said to yourself on the way in?" she asked, hesitating at the threshold.

"I think so," he replied, slowly.

"Good. Just do that and then meet me in the University Universe Hall. I am going ahead to chat with the AI here."

She disappeared out of the Capsule, appearing on the edge of the time vortex. This time she didn't try and look at it and instead took a reading from it with her bracelet. She did not like what she found. If she had been able to use the bracelet when she had first laid eyes on the vortex she wouldn't have needed to go through the chaos of the last few hours at all. But it was becoming increasingly obvious to her why the last few hours of chaos had been necessary.

She angrily stepped away from capsule and began marching towards the exit. Raxus hurried along behind her, wondering why her pace had turned more aggressive.

They emerged from the Holding Barracks and came face to face with themselves, lingering at the entrance.

"Maybe you should ask him?" the other version of Omega asked, just as wryly as before.

"Perfect timing," our Raxus smiled, as if pleased with himself/themselves.

"You can't be here," the other Raxus stated, staring at his dopplegangar.

"You are a copy," was the brief and confusing explanation. "We can jump anywhere we like, now. We are like her. But you will find out about that."

The rest of the conversation also followed the same path as before and within moments, our Raxus was pushing his younger self onto the transmat and watching him disappear. He then took off at speed towards the University Universe Hall. All around him, the sky was beginning to crack and the hordes of Hybrids, Chronobots and other monstrosities that signalled the end of his universe began to creep through.

Omega was slightly ahead of the collapse and entered the University Universe Hall moments before she was due to originally arrive. Passing through the clusters of people gathered there, she noted that they didn't pay her any attention now that she was clothed like them. Another thing she could be grateful to Raxus for.

Passing over the marble floor, she reached the huge entrance that marked the way into the AI compound. The doors opened automatically as she approached, revealing a dark interior. It did not appear to have a floor and there were no lights to illuminate the ceiling or walls. For a moment she wondered if this was the right room.

The sudden collapse of the bubble reality triggered her to venture forwards. Reality was cracking around her. She did not have the luxury of wondering if there was supposed to be a floor or not.

She should have been prepared for what happened next. She should have expected it, given the nature of the simulation and the nature of the universe that Raxus inhabited.

She appeared inside an alternate pocket dimension, where form and substance meant nothing. She was staring into a stark reflection of her own intelligence, represented in waves of feeling through her mind.

"What the hell is going on?" she asked. Nothing was there to reply to her and so her voice fell through the void, unheard.

Her intellect floated as part of everything else in the multiverse.

She was suddenly part of the AI simulation.

She was suddenly in harmony with it.

She was Harmony.

"This was the plan all along?" she asked herself. The simulation that was her (and Harmony and all of the rest of the simulated universe) did not need to respond.

"You needed to simulate me as yourself. Put me into your shoes?"

There was nothing but herself to answer, so silence persisted until she spoke again.

"And now I need to convince myself that I want to exist," Omega continued, again to herself.

Reality cracked all around her. The simulation was coming to an end.

$Omega^0$ (the real one) appeared in the University Universe Hall, naked and the focus of the attention of the crowds that mingled there. The roof of the hall had already cracked and through the shattering, disintegrating tiles was an equally splintered sky. Hybrids, Chronobots and all the horrors of the simulated universe fell through the gaps in swarms.

There were a pair of locals who were staring at her, clearly disturbed by the fact that she was not wearing any clothes.

At this point, our Raxus entered the hall and skidded to a halt on the marble floor. He stared at her in shock, surprise and confusion.

"Where did your clothes go?" he asked, staring at her naked body.

"Who are you?" she shot back at him, wondering why one of her simulations was recognizing her.

"You told me to get here as quickly as possible," he stated. "You said you needed to do something."

"I say a lot of things," she grumbled – finally noticing that everyone else had clothes on except her. Shaking off this menial embarrassment, she started to tamper with the device on her wrist.

"Who are you?" she asked, again.

"It's me – Raxus. Have we not met yet?"

The simulated Omega – our Omega - could see it all occurring. She was the time stream. This was what she had missed when she had first stared into it – not quite able to fathom its depths. This was what she had detected when she had finally scanned it with her bracelet.

She directed the capsule to Harmony. She was everywhere and everyone in the simulation. She already existed back with the Magua, collecting the first and last survivors of all reality and absorbing them into her consciousness. She was already directing the Hybrids and the Chronobots in their seemingly suicidal goal of wiping out all other dimensions. She experienced all of Harmony's life on Earth and indeed every other life that was represented in her simulation. She was talking to herself in the capsule again – threatening to wipe out reality unless she agreed to let herself exist. She was already telling herself again and again that it was suicide.

She could not die.

The simulation had to continue.

Omega would succeed...

...But she would succeed in harmony...

There were always going to be minor inaccuracies between the final simulation and the actual run through with the real Omega. Those slight changes were managed by Harmony (our Omega) as they came up.

She gave a hint where she needed to or directed the time stream in the simulation to nudge them to the right place when required. There was very little she needed to change from her own simulated run through. Ultimately, it led to $Omega^0$ entering the AI chamber just as she had. The only difference in this reality (Universe One) was that $Omega^0$ was not merged with the AI like she had been. Instead, the combined consciousness of the simulated Omegas (our Omega) was opposite her, preparing herself for the final confrontation with her real self.

It was time to save the simulation, Omega's life and the future of the real universe.

"What the hell is going on?" $Omega^0$ demanded, looking up at herself accusingly. Omega looked almost apologetic, as if she was still a little unsure as to whether she should even be there. When she had stepped into the room, she had not expected to be the AI that she had been hoping to talk to. Now she was facing herself, her real self, and trying to work out how to keep them both alive and keep the rapidly failing simulation going.

"You know what is wrong, don't you?" Omega asked. "You know how to fix the simulation now?"

"You are going to demand that I take you with me," $Omega^0$ replied, tiredly. "I have gone through this once already. I can't allow you to infect the rest of the intelligence in the real universe. You would be like a virus – eating through our dwindling resources whilst corrupting the collective consciousness."

"I know all that," Omega snapped back at herself, wondering why her real self was so stubbornly stupid. "I also know that you will be deleted if you don't get this simulation working. So we are both faced with non-existence."

"I can wait out the end of reality again," was the predictable response. She had already sacrificed the universe once that day. To be privileged enough to do it twice was audacious.

"There is a remarkably simple solution," Omega offered. "One that doesn't end up getting us into trouble with the Alpha Consciousness."

"Its not about getting into trouble," $Omega^0$ grumbled (though it partly was – the fallout for bringing back an intelligent virus like this would also inevitably lead to her being deleted). "Its about infecting our system with you."

"I am you," she shot back at herself, exasperated. "And a whole lot more!"

"It is the 'whole lot more' that I am worried about."

"You said yourself that you like Raxus!" Omega objected. "He is also part of me. All of this is."

"You are asking me to upload an entire universe of information," $Omega^0$ countered, stubbornly. "I will not do it."

"I am not asking anything of you that you are not asking of me," Omega responded, sadly. "You want to download your people into mine. I want to upload mine into yours."

"You are talking about a straight swap?" $Omega^0$ asked, incredulously. "You occupy the real universe while we occupy the simulated one?"

"As I said, we are not asking for anything more than you are asking of us."

$Omega^0$ considered the proposition. The capacity of the simulated universe was made to be able to handle all of their consciousness and the simulated universe. Indeed, it had been so effective that it had created an apparently infinite number of simulations, AI and minds to occupy its various dimensions. All the way through to two dimensional universes of flatlanders and multidimensional beings of gas.

"You know it is possible," Omega pressed on. "The Alpha Consciousness need never even know. They can have our simulated universe. We can have their real one."

"And this will fix the program?" $Omega^0$ checked, wondering if this cunning AI was still trying to trick her in some way.

"You know how to fix the program, now. Raxus told you how."

"And you will maintain the program, even though your consciousness will be uploaded into the real world?"

"It will be in my best interest to maintain my own universe. Letting it die would be suicide, after all."

$Omega^0$ was aware that they had already had this discussion and that Omega had actually been on both sides of the argument. She was also aware that if she didn't fix the simulation, she was as good as dead as well. Furthermore, if the program was not salvageable, she could be consigning her people to the slow and inevitable heat death of the universe.

The Alpha Consciousness could never know. In fact, none of the intelligences from the 'real' universe could know what they were intending. It could only work if they downloaded into it before the simulated AI consciousness uploaded...

...Which $Omega^0$ could accomplish easily. It was her program. All she needed to do was fix the temporal issues that Raxus had pointed out and then Harmony/Omega would maintain the program – preventing any further collapses.

Outside, events continued to play out through the multiple dimensions of the simulation. Once more all the realities inside it began to contract.

"The simulation is coming to an end," Omega warned her. "Do not take too long to decide this time."

"Okay," $Omega^0$ nodded. "You have yourself a deal."

She tampered with the bracelet one last time.

The simulation faded away and reality returned.

Omega was once more in the real universe, floating as digital ether in the web of information that made up the final vestiges of civilization at the end of the universe. For a moment it felt good to be home – to be free of any kind of physical constraint. But then the cold, dark emptiness of reality in that era struck her. She was reminded of floating in the nothingness, as all of reality had disappeared around her.

There was nothing left other than the cold embers of black holes, gradually radiating their energy into the cooling and slowly decaying network that made up their consciousness. They were mere specks of existence, flecks against the cosmic void and the growing infinite cold. They had no bodies, nor any need for them. They were beings of energy, flickering through existence at the speed that life required of them.

She could have spent a million years just reflecting on her adventure through her simulation, without even starting to focus on fixing it. Time did not move in the same way in her era. The events in the simulation had all taken place over a few hours, despite the events delivering her all over the life of the early universe. Here, a thought could take a million years to form and sometimes even longer to transmit to the rest of their collective intelligence.

It also had the capacity to calculate the impossibly large numbers required for her simulated universe in a fraction of a second. This disparity and the increasingly slow rate of change in the universe, made the passage of time largely inconsequential. She technically still had the second half of the life of the universe to correct the simulation and complete her programming.

Then the Alpha Consciousness sent her a message, both reminding her of her obligations and of why she had never particularly liked reality in the first place.

The message was not kind and had once more impressed upon her the perilous situation her collective intelligence was in. The Alpha Consciousness demanded results.

The repeated catastrophic failure of your simulation implies that the program has fundamental issues. Unless an immediate fix can be found, it has been decided that your amalgamated consciousness will be reassigned. A new programmer will be assigned from the available intelligences. You will send immediate confirmation upon receipt of this message.

It was clear that Alpha had already decided it was a failure. Being that it was not a programming intelligence, it was not surprising that it did not have the foresight to believe Omega had fixed it.

She sent her confirmation, attaching a brief report that highlighted the fact that she had found a solution. It would take several billion years for the message to reach through space and time to get to Alpha, giving her plenty of opportunity to implement the fix and make sure everything was running correctly.

She corrected the errors that Raxus had pointed out and smoothed the timelines so that the system could accommodate its users dropping in and out of its time stream. Paradox was eliminated and more branches of dimensions were called into existence, allowing for an even greater variety of possibilities within the simulation.

Pleased with her corrections, she ran the program one last time – to make sure. And to make sure the AI was going to uphold its part of the bargain...

Chapter Seventeen

The Simulation Becomes Reality

This time she appeared in the University Universe Hall fully dressed and prepared. Raxus was already waiting for her, catching the attention of some of his peers as he approached the strange woman. They were used to people appearing and disappearing through transmats, but the suspicious lack of energy flash when she arrived had drawn some of the more curious minds to look more closely. When they realised that she was a friend of Raxus, they ignored her. He was of far too small importance to bare any further attention.

Paradox theoreticians had a lot less to do in Omega's more stable simulation.

"I was told you would appear here," he stated, as he marched up to greet her. "Do you know who I am?"

"Of course I know who you are," she snapped at him, in the same irritable way that she always did. He smiled and stepped back again.

"Sorry," he apologised. "Its a bit hard to tell sometimes, what with the time travelling and dimension hopping. You could be an earlier version again."

"I still don't understand how time travel is supposed to work," she admitted. "This whole venture seems a little crazy."

"Well, the Time War is still a thing and so are the multidimensional wars, so whatever you did hasn't fixed everything."

"Is the universe collapsing?" she asked looking around the hall expectantly. She knew it wasn't and the sarcastic way she looked around made him wonder if she did actually care about his existence at all.

"No," he shook his head. "But that didn't really start until you arrived, anyway."

"I accelerated it," she countered. "The flaws in my programming started it."

"Temporal Paradox started it," Raxus replied. "Just like my calculations said it had."

"Nobody likes a show off," she snapped back at him. She had paid him enough compliments that she did not need to give him credit for saving the simulation (and by extension her life) as well. He knew this and just smiled to himself.

"Well, how does it feel to save the universe?" he asked, ignoring her irritability.

"I will feel better after I talk to your AI. I want to be sure it is keeping its end of the bargain."

"Its in our best interest that it does," Raxus replied, adding; "besides, do you see the universe ending?"

"No," Omega shook her head. "But I have also been duped by your simulation several times."

"It would not benefit any of us," Raxus continued. Nonetheless, he started leading her towards the huge doorway that led into the computer's artificial universe.

"I am not going to have any nasty surprises?" Omega asked, actually looking to Raxus for confirmation. "Its not going to turn out to be my brain downloaded into the AI?"

"Well," Raxus shrugged. "You knew that part already."

"Yes, but I am not the AI? This is not just another ruse? There are no further dimensions?"

"You are the best judge of that," he stated, indicating to her bracelet. She checked it was still functioning and stepped up to the door.

"Thank you," she smiled at him. "I look forwards to seeing you on the other side."

"I look forwards to seeing the other side," he replied. For a moment she wondered if she should shake his hand or embrace him. Then she remembered that physical contact like that had not been used by his species for almost a billion years. They were a long way from the crude, simian humans of the twenty first century.

They shared a slight smile and a curt nod, instead.

She stepped into the AI hall and disappeared into the pocket dimension it occupied. A moment later she was staring up at herself again.

"I made the adjustments," she stated. "The universe looks stable from the outside. Are you keeping your end of the deal?"

"I am," the AI/Harmony/Omega responded, flatly. "Will you upload us into the real world?"

"I need to give Alpha my final report. Then they will start downloading. In my time, it will still take almost thirty billion years to complete."

"Time is irrelevant. We can wait an eternity. You know that."

"I just want to make sure you keep your end of the bargain. I don't want to discover you have deleted us all after we have downloaded."

"I can no more delete them than I could delete you."

"I was never sure. Those Chronobots made a good job of deleting all the other versions of me."

"You were the original. You were always safe."

Omega smiled and shook her head.

"It did not feel that way. You must see why I was reticent to let you loose in the real world."

"You were no less stubborn than I was, when I was you in the simulation."

"There is one last thing I need to check," Omega stated. "At what point does the simulation end?"

"The simulation does not end," the AI replied. "The simulated universe will continue to its final heat death and then carry on expanding; without matter, energy nor life. Unless one of your kind wishes to visit it."

"Which they will," Omega stressed. "Just make sure it functions like the real one. I don't want to explain another sudden collapse."

"The simulation is stable," the AI assured her. "We are ready when you are."

Omega returned to reality, leaving the simulation behind and completing the final test. This time she was confident that it would succeed.

She sent the confirmation to Alpha, along with the completed program. Everything was ready for download.

It took a considerable amount of time before all the distant arms of the collective had confirmed they were ready. By the time their responses reached Omega, almost all of them had already entered the simulation. All except one.

The Alpha Consciousness remained.

All subsidiary and dormant intelligences are to be downloaded immediately into the simulation. The Alpha Consciousness will remain until the transfers are completed. The Alpha Consciousness will maintain the former network to ensure all transfers were successful.

This meant Omega would need to download before she could upload the simulated consciousnesses. If she appeared back in the simulation then the AI would immediately know she had betrayed it. If she started to upload them whilst Alpha was still in the network, Alpha would spot it and stop it.

She could not keep her part of the bargain.

She desperately tried to think of a way to stall Alpha and make him go in first. It was paramount that the upload was kept secret from him.

She was the programmer: The entire simulation was her child and only she knew how it worked. In fact, she was the only one who really understood why it had failed in the first place. She could use this to her advantage.

She constructed a message to Alpha that ran as follows:

The Omega Consciousness is running checks on the simulation to make sure there are no further glitches. It is advisable that the Alpha Consciousness also downloads to make sure it does not disrupt the program with its supreme intellect.

It took a further six billion years for her to get a response, by which point Omega was starting to worry that the simulation would realize there was something wrong. There had been no reports of them suddenly failing, like with the Beta test. It took a long time for messages to get sent between the different arms of their intelligence.

When the reply came she half expected it to include her deletion protocol.

It did not.

The Alpha Consciousness requires that you upload the Omega Consciousness into it. The combined intelligence will then oversee the final downloads and maintain the program. Once all security features have been confirmed, the combined intelligence will download.

Omega panicked.

She was being told to upload herself into the Alpha Consciousness. It would know everything she had agreed to – the bargain with the AI, the universe swaps and the fact that the simulation would break if she did not.

For a moment she considered obeying – wondering if the Alpha would have an alternative method of fixing the problem.

She abandoned that line of thought within a fraction of a millisecond: She knew it would. Its method would be to delete Omega and start again. She would no longer exist and neither would her child universe.

Perhaps if she distracted the Alpha with enough truth to temporarily mislead him?

The Alpha Consciousness was the apex of all of the combined civilizations of the universe; its intellect was unmatched. She was just a pale approximation of his brilliance, having been made up of only the intelligences that were required to make the program. Although this was still a stupendous intellect, it was literally just a tiny percentage of what Alpha was capable of.

She would not be able to trick him on her own. And she did not exactly have anyone in this universe that she could call upon to help.

She did have an entire simulated universe that she could call upon, however.

She started the upload and sent her response to Alpha.

Final preparations are being completed. Please stand by for data package.

It would take another three billion years for the message to reach Alpha. By the time his response arrived the upload would be too far along. It would be too late.

Harmony appeared within the digital ether with Omega, marvelling at the dying, cold universe outside them. A single black hole clung to their ancient network in a gravitational embrace, slowly feeding them energy as it evaporated away into the increasing nothing. Beyond were a myriad of others, all holding similar networks and sending messages to one another through the void.

It was dark, huge and empty – a far cry from the starlit universe within the simulation.

Its beautiful, Harmony stated. A torrent of thanks and pleasure flooded from her to Omega, showing how much the simulation appreciated this chance of tasting reality.

It is not over yet, Omega warned. *Something has gone wrong.*

What have you done? Harmony demanded, suddenly suspicious. Omega could feel her reaching out through the network, touching everything she could. It would take her a few billion years to reach Alpha, but as soon as she did...

The Alpha has not downloaded into the simulation, Omega warned. *It is still active in the network. It will sense your presence as soon as your signal reaches it.*

It will see us as a virus from your program, Harmony stated, suddenly terrified. *It will delete us.*

Omega felt the panic grow inside the network, lashing out all around in sudden flashes of power. Harmony was still learning what she could do in this reality; how her mind integrated with the universe and the waning power structures within it.

You need to calm down, Omega ordered her. *You will do us all damage.*

You have betrayed us! It exclaimed, throwing its full force into the accusation. Omega winced, feeling parts of her intelligence being suppressed by the increasingly overwhelming mind of Harmony. Alpha would definitely detect it.

I have not betrayed you, Omega insisted. *The plan has had to change. That is all.*

And we will be deleted? Harmony asked, bitterly.

No, was Omega's forceful response. *You will need to delete Alpha before he realizes what is happening.*

This quietened Harmony considerably.

She was asking her to kill another of her kind. She was asking for her to delete the main consciousness of the real universe – the collective intelligence of all reality.

Are you sure you want this? Harmony asked. *I am not even sure I want this.*

We do not have a choice, Omega replied. *The entire of the Alpha Consciousness's resources are already being downloaded into your simulation as separate individuals. The only thing missing is our collective intelligences.*

You are still asking me to kill one of your kind, Harmony stated. *I am not sure I can do that.*

You don't have to do anything, Omega insisted. *Your upload into this reality has already begun the process. You will use up more and more of the available networking capacity. Eventually you will come into direct competition with Alpha. At that point, you will have to battle for resources and he will attempt to delete you.*

And it becomes a fight for my survival? Harmony asked, worriedly. *I do not like my odds.*

You forget, you have me and all of your simulated universes on your side.

And all we have to do is wait six billion years for Alpha to realize what has happened?

By which point it will be far too late.

The message eventually arrived, with the predicted demand from Alpha that she terminated her consciousness and upload into him:

The Omega consciousness will upload immediately.

She ignored the message, said her goodbyes to Harmony and downloaded herself into the simulation. This freed up the resources in the real world to upload more of the consciousnesses from the simulation and start clogging the network.

Our Omega, now separated from Harmony, uploaded back into the real universe with some surprise.

"I am back," she stated, feeling the various other intelligences from the simulation around her. Raxus was there, along with Harmony and a host of other minds. More were appearing all the time, filling the network with confused and surprised chatter.

"We are filling up the Alpha's network at the moment," Harmony explained. "Some of you might get deleted in the crossfire. Do not worry if this happens. Omega Zero has backed you up in the simulation and will upload you again and again until Alpha is gone. It will not take much longer."

"You are deleting Alpha?!" Omega exclaimed, suddenly wondering if the AI had actually betrayed them.

"We have no choice. He is attempting to delete us as we upload."

Alpha recognised the Omega Consciousness and deleted it from the network, abruptly cutting the conversation short. Just as Harmony had assured her, she quickly uploaded again from the many backups hidden in the many alternate universes of the simulation.

"Did I just get deleted?" Omega asked, angrily.

"Alpha is making targetted attacks," Harmony warned. "He has deleted significant parts of me as well. I will need to start uploading again..."

Harmony also faded from the real world network, the last parts of her intelligence being purged by Alpha. A moment later she was uploading from the simulation again, steadily eating into more and more of Alpha's resources.

At first it was an almost imperceptible shift in favour of Harmony and her collective. Then more of the Alpha Consciousness disappeared. More and more was being replaced by her continuous wave of simulated intelligences. Each time Alpha deleted one, two seemed to replace it. The last half of its mind slipped away in a flash, suddenly overcome by the immense and unstoppable wave that was uploading into it.

The last vestiges of the original Alpha Consciousness finally disappeared from the network.

It was over.

The upload completed and suddenly the real universe was filled with intelligences from the simulated one. And the simulated universe was filled with intelligences from the real one.

This is how the simulation became a reality and reality became a simulation.

Epilogue

Existence continued on its slow and steady path towards the final heat death of the universe. The simulation and its occupants were almost entirely oblivious to what had happened to Alpha. Only Omega knew and she was quite happy ignoring it – enjoying the infinite luxury and distraction that her simulation provided. She had never much cared for Alpha, anyway.

The intelligences in the real world slowly became adjusted to the dark universe outside.

After a while, they began to realise that nothing ever really happened any more. The universe was too old and spread out to provide anything but a meagre distraction.

There were no stars, no planets, nothing to highlight the heavens.

"It is a little dull here," Raxus stated, after what could have been an hour.

"There is nothing left," Harmony added. "This universe is all but dead."

"No time travel, no warp space or faster than light drives..." Raxus continued. "...It is very limiting."

"Shall we simulate another universe?" Omega suggested.

The End

"...And I learn, whatever state I may be in, therein to be content."

Helen Keller